BLACK PANTHER

A NATION UNDER OUR FEET: PART 9

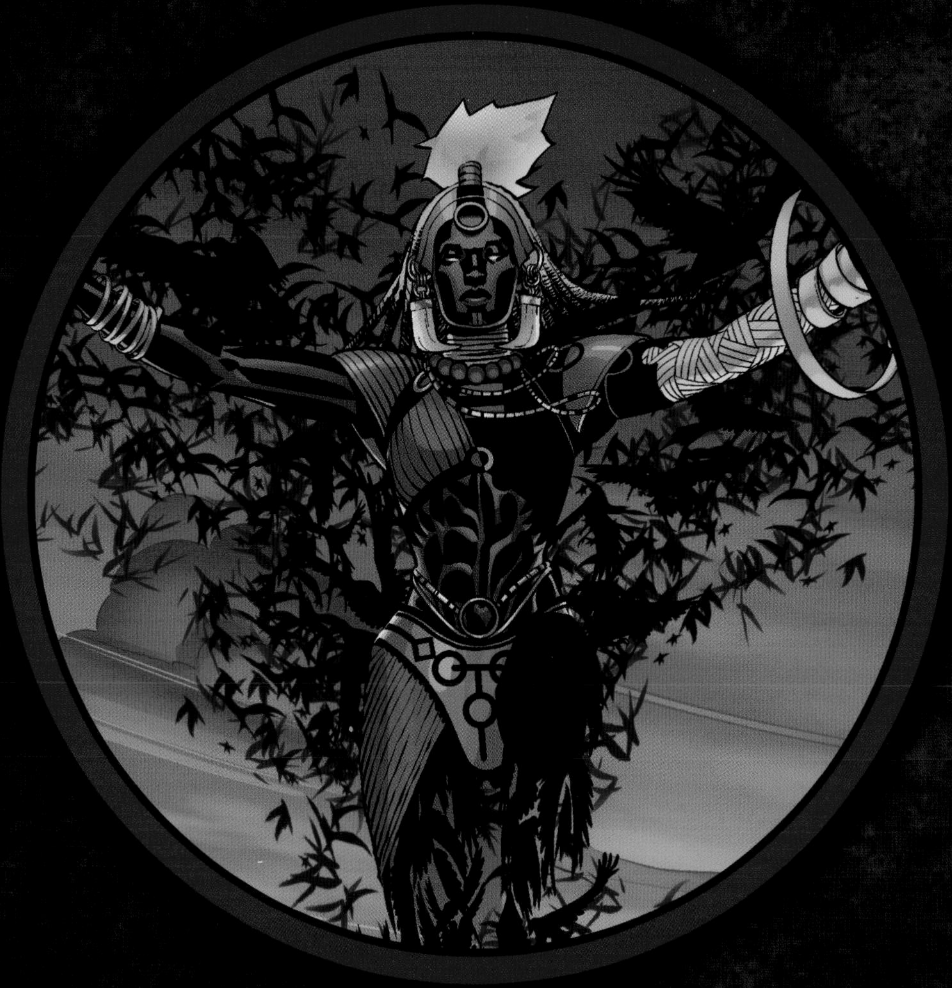

MARVEL

ABDOBOOKS.COM

Reinforced library bound edition published in 2021 by Spotlight,
a division of ABDO, PO Box 398166, Minneapolis, Minnesota 55439.
Spotlight produces high-quality reinforced library bound editions for
schools and libraries. Published by agreement with Marvel Characters, Inc.

Printed in the United States of America, North Mankato, Minnesota.
092020
012021

THIS BOOK CONTAINS
RECYCLED MATERIALS

© 2021 MARVEL

Library of Congress Control Number: 2020942382

Publisher's Cataloging-in-Publication Data

Names: Coates, Ta-Nehisi, author. | Sprouse, Chris; Story, Karl; Martin, Laura; Wong,
    Walden; Stelfreeze, Brian; Hanna, Scott, illustrators.
Title: A nation under our feet / by Ta-Nehisi Coates; illustrated by Chris Sprouse,
    Karl Story, Laura Martin, Walden Wong, Brian Stelfreeze and Scott Hanna.
Description: Minneapolis, Minnesota: Spotlight, 2021 | Series: Black panther
Summary: With a dramatic upheaval in Wakanda on the horizon, T'Challa knows his
    kingdom needs to change to survive, but he struggles to find balance in his
    roles as king and the Black Panther.
Identifiers: ISBN 9781532147784 (pt. 7, lib. bdg.) | ISBN 9781532147791 (pt. 8, lib.
    bdg.) | ISBN 9781532147807 (pt. 9, lib. bdg.) | ISBN 9781532147814 (pt. 10,
    lib. bdg.) | ISBN 9781532147821 (pt. 11, lib. bdg.) | ISBN 9781532147838 (pt.
    12, lib. bdg.)
Subjects: LCSH: Black Panther (Fictitious character)--Juvenile fiction. | Superheroes--
    Juvenile fiction. | Kings and rulers--Juvenile fiction. | Graphic novels--Juvenile
    fiction. | T'Challa, of Wakanda (Fictitious character)--Juvenile fiction.
Classification: DDC 741.5--dc23

Spotlight

A Division of ABDO
abdobooks.com

BLACK PANTHER

SINCE THANOS'S ATTACK ON WAKANDA, **SHURI**—FORMER QUEEN, FORMER BLACK PANTHER, AND SISTER TO T'CHALLA—HAD BEEN TRAPPED IN A PETRIFIED STATE KNOWN AS **THE LIVING DEATH**. HER SPIRIT WAS DRIVEN TO **THE DJALIA**, THE PLANE OF WAKANDAN MEMORY. WHILE THERE, SHE LEARNED OF WAKANDA'S PAST, PRESENT, AND FUTURE FROM A GRIOT WEARING THE ASPECT OF HER MOTHER, RAMONDA. MEANWHILE, THE REAL RAMONDA IS UNDER INTENSIVE MEDICAL CARE DUE TO INJURIES SHE RECEIVED DURING A SUICIDE BOMBING.

AFTER MONTHS OF AGONIZING RESEARCH AND EXPERIMENTATION IN AN EFFORT TO REVIVE HIS SISTER, **T'CHALLA** CONSTRUCTED A TRANSVERSE DIMENSIONAL BRACE TO AUGMENT **MANIFOLD'S** TELEPORTATION ABILITIES AND SEND THEIR SPIRITS TO THE DJALIA TO RETRIEVE HER. SHURI RETURNED TO THE PHYSICAL PLANE WITH WAKANDA'S COLLECTIVE KNOWLEDGE AND NEW ABILITIES.

MEANWHILE, A REBELLION RAVAGES WAKANDA. A FACTION KNOWN AS **THE PEOPLE**, LED BY **TETU** AND **ZENZI**, GATHERS FORCES TO TOPPLE T'CHALLA'S REGIME. THE DORA MILAJE, FORMERLY THE PROTECTION SERVICE TO THE CROWN, HAVE BROKEN AWAY UNDER THE DIRECTION OF **THE MIDNIGHT ANGELS**—AYO AND **ANEKA**—TO PROTECT AND SERVE IGNORED WAKANDANS WHILE T'CHALLA'S ATTENTION HAS BEEN SPREAD THIN. THE PEOPLE AND THE DORA MILAJE AGREE THAT WAKANDA NEEDS NEW LEADERSHIP, BUT HAVE NOT YET MADE A FORMAL ALLIANCE...

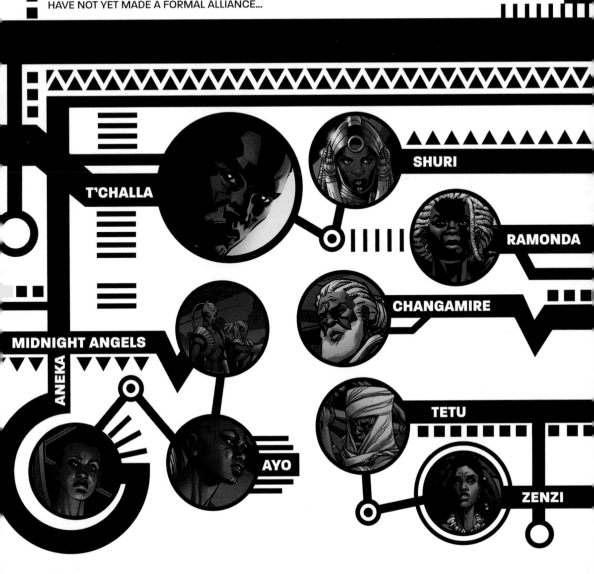

T'CHALLA

SHURI

RAMONDA

CHANGAMIRE

MIDNIGHT ANGELS

ANEKA

AYO

TETU

ZENZI

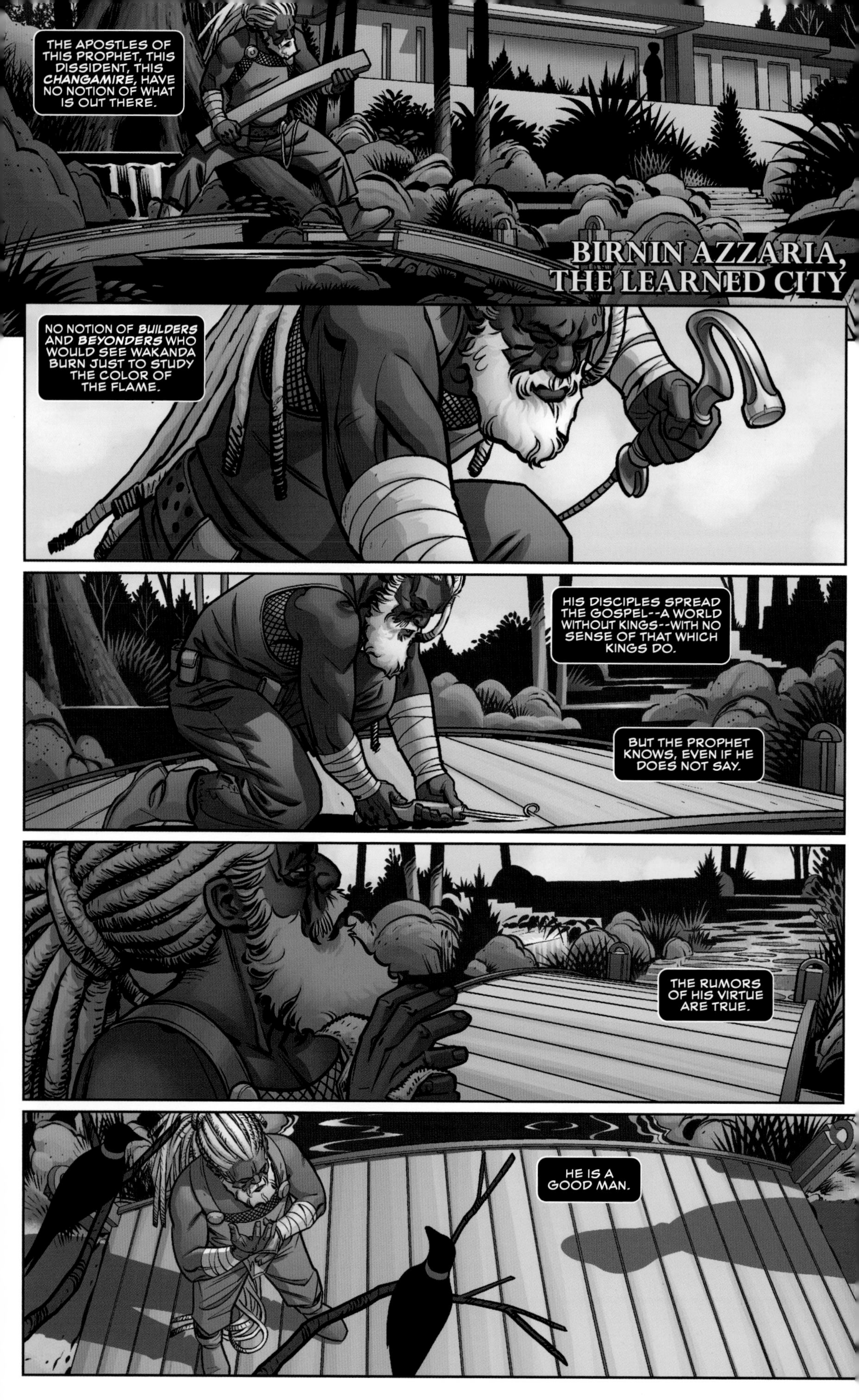
THE APOSTLES OF THIS PROPHET, THIS DISSIDENT, THIS CHANGAMIRE, HAVE NO NOTION OF WHAT IS OUT THERE.
BIRNIN AZZARIA, THE LEARNED CITY
NO NOTION OF BUILDERS AND BEYONDERS WHO WOULD SEE WAKANDA BURN JUST TO STUDY THE COLOR OF THE FLAME.
HIS DISCIPLES SPREAD THE GOSPEL--A WORLD WITHOUT KINGS--WITH NO SENSE OF THAT WHICH KINGS DO.
BUT THE PROPHET KNOWS, EVEN IF HE DOES NOT SAY.
THE RUMORS OF HIS VIRTUE ARE TRUE.
HE IS A GOOD MAN.

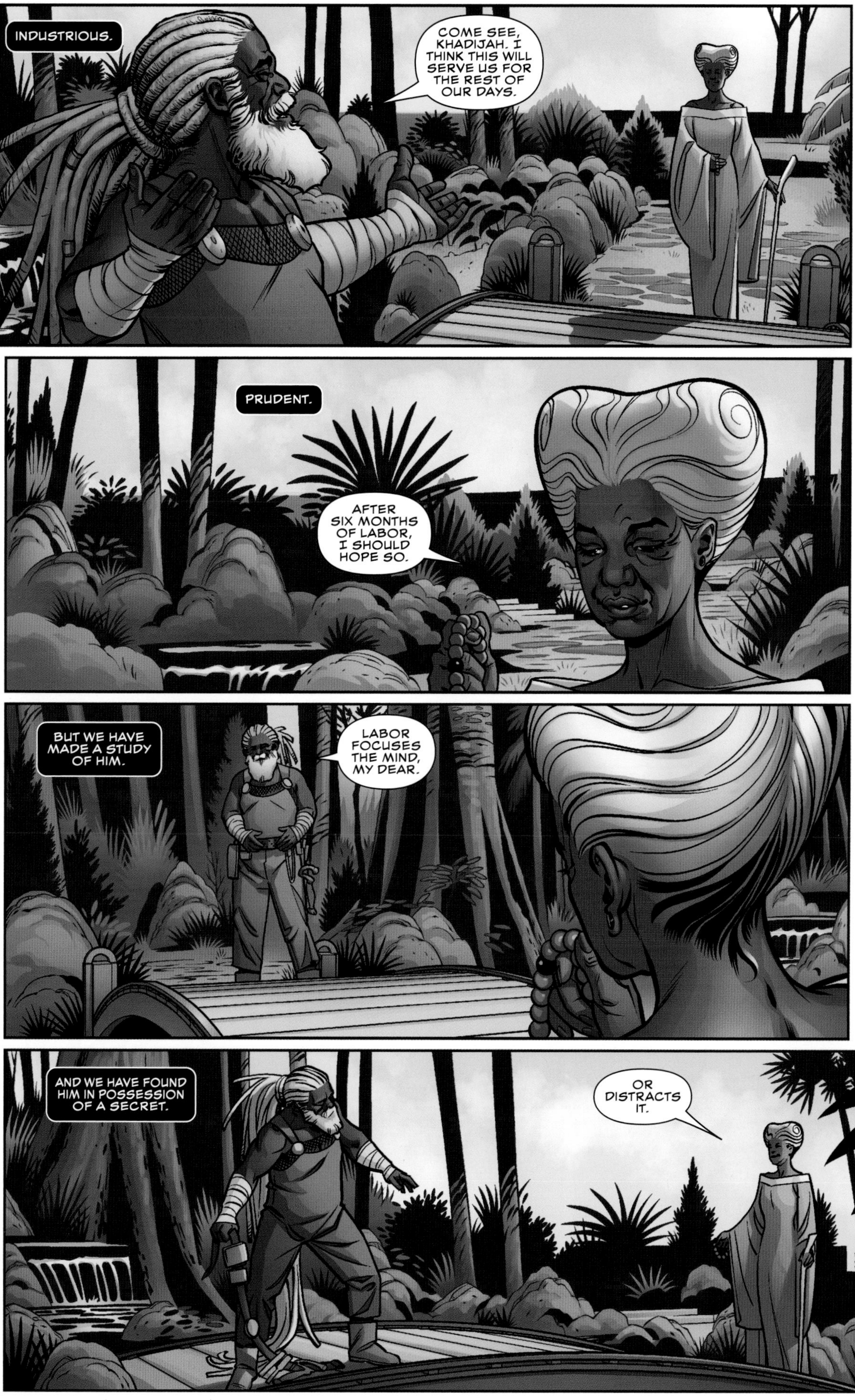
INDUSTRIOUS.
COME SEE, KHADIJAH. I THINK THIS WILL SERVE US FOR THE REST OF OUR DAYS.
PRUDENT.
AFTER SIX MONTHS OF LABOR, I SHOULD HOPE SO.
BUT WE HAVE MADE A STUDY OF HIM.
LABOR FOCUSES THE MIND, MY DEAR.
AND WE HAVE FOUND HIM IN POSSESSION OF A SECRET.
OR DISTRACTS IT.

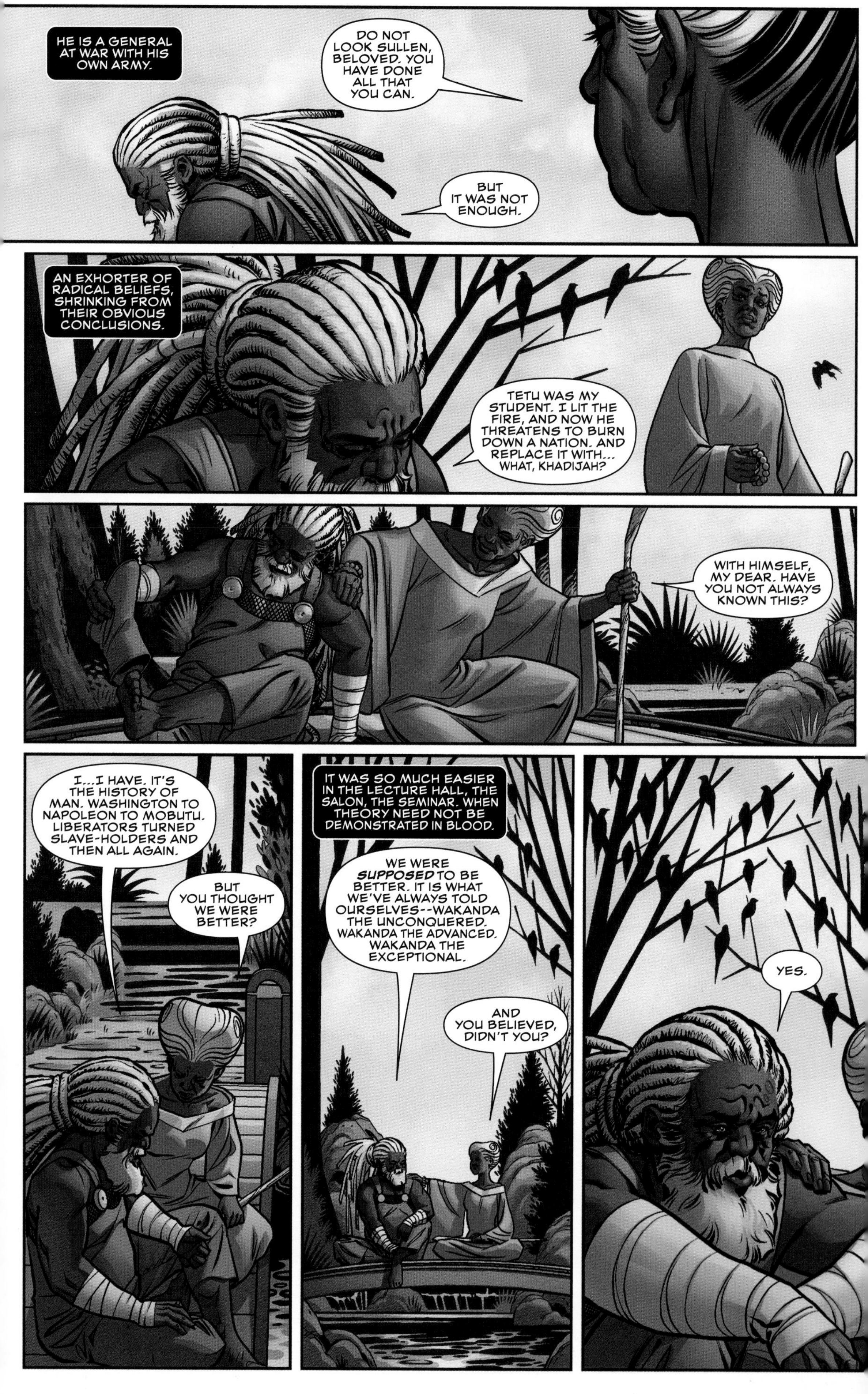
HE IS A GENERAL AT WAR WITH HIS OWN ARMY.
DO NOT LOOK SULLEN, BELOVED. YOU HAVE DONE ALL THAT YOU CAN.
BUT IT WAS NOT ENOUGH.
AN EXHORTER OF RADICAL BELIEFS, SHRINKING FROM THEIR OBVIOUS CONCLUSIONS.
TETU WAS MY STUDENT. I LIT THE FIRE, AND NOW HE THREATENS TO BURN DOWN A NATION. AND REPLACE IT WITH... WHAT, KHADIJAH?
WITH HIMSELF, MY DEAR. HAVE YOU NOT ALWAYS KNOWN THIS?
I...I HAVE. IT'S THE HISTORY OF MAN. WASHINGTON TO NAPOLEON TO MOBUTU. LIBERATORS TURNED SLAVE-HOLDERS AND THEN ALL AGAIN.
BUT YOU THOUGHT WE WERE BETTER?
IT WAS SO MUCH EASIER IN THE LECTURE HALL, THE SALON, THE SEMINAR. WHEN THEORY NEED NOT BE DEMONSTRATED IN BLOOD.
WE WERE *SUPPOSED* TO BE BETTER. IT IS WHAT WE'VE ALWAYS TOLD OURSELVES--WAKANDA THE UNCONQUERED. WAKANDA THE ADVANCED. WAKANDA THE EXCEPTIONAL.
AND YOU BELIEVED, DIDN'T YOU?
YES.

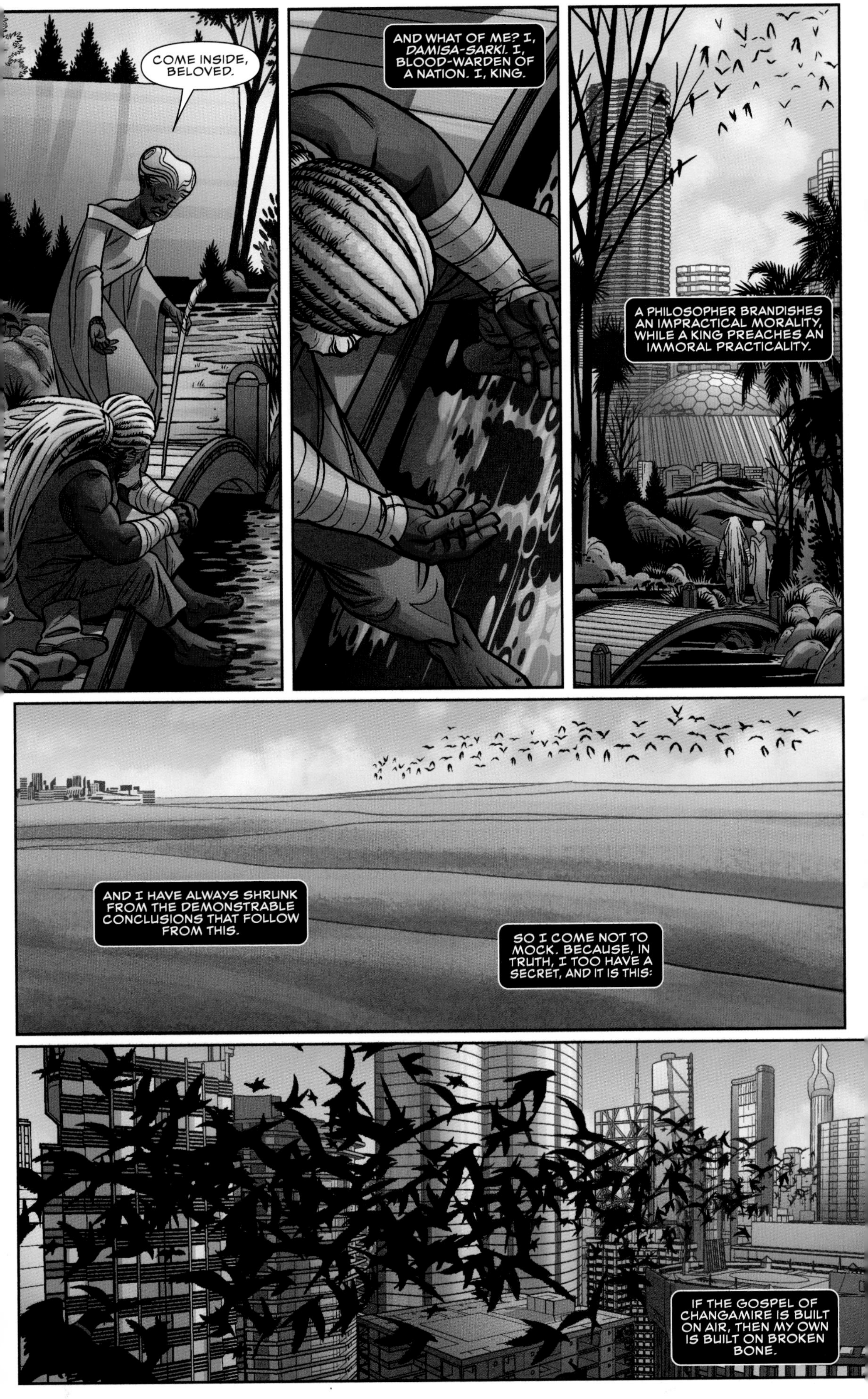
COME INSIDE, BELOVED.
AND WHAT OF ME? I, DAMISA-SARKI. I, BLOOD-WARDEN OF A NATION. I, KING.
A PHILOSOPHER BRANDISHES AN IMPRACTICAL MORALITY, WHILE A KING PREACHES AN IMMORAL PRACTICALITY.
AND I HAVE ALWAYS SHRUNK FROM THE DEMONSTRABLE CONCLUSIONS THAT FOLLOW FROM THIS.
SO I COME NOT TO MOCK. BECAUSE, IN TRUTH, I TOO HAVE A SECRET, AND IT IS THIS:
IF THE GOSPEL OF CHANGAMIRE IS BUILT ON AIR, THEN MY OWN IS BUILT ON BROKEN BONE.

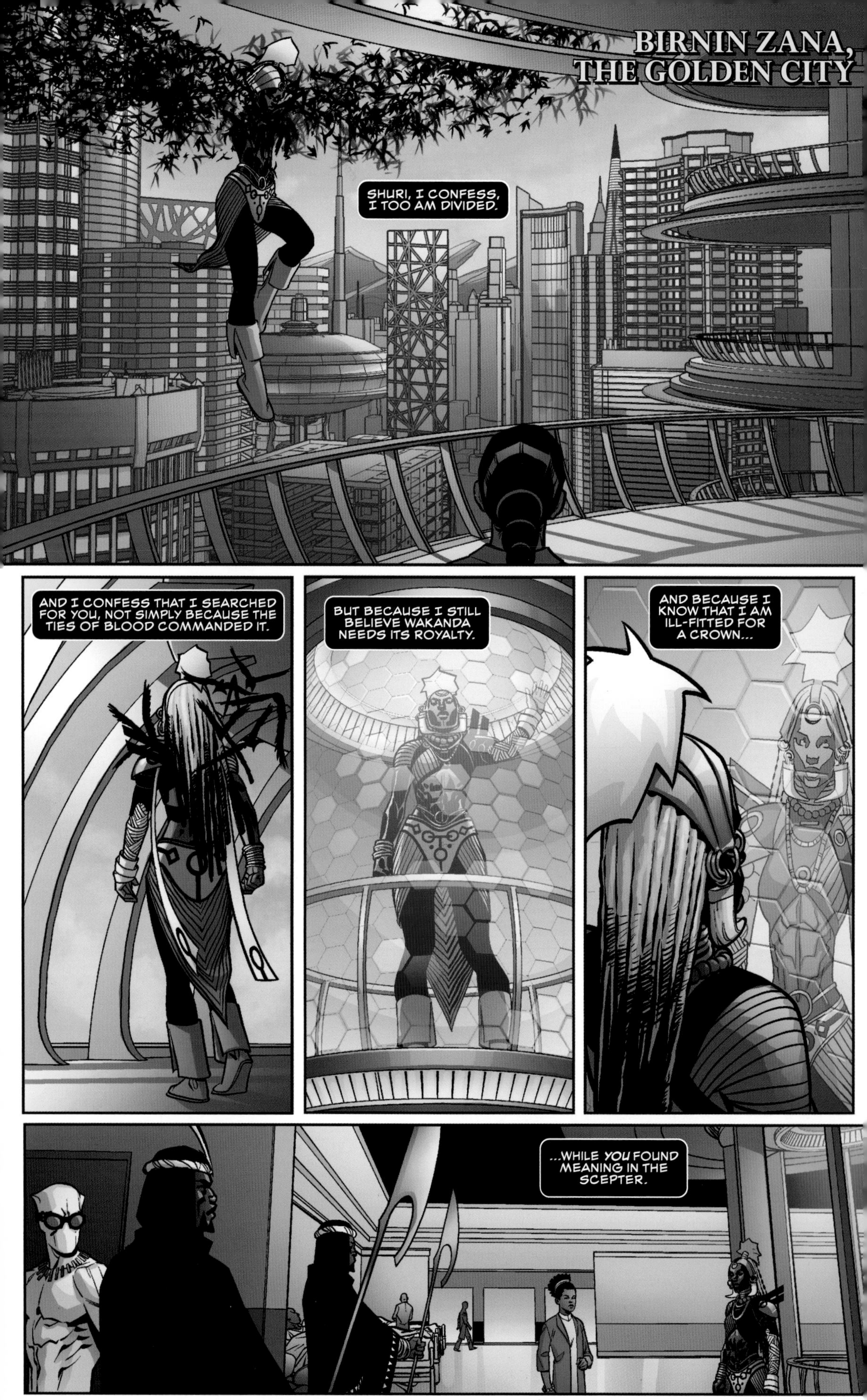
BIRNIN ZANA, THE GOLDEN CITY
SHURI, I CONFESS, I TOO AM DIVIDED.
AND I CONFESS THAT I SEARCHED FOR YOU, NOT SIMPLY BECAUSE THE TIES OF BLOOD COMMANDED IT.
BUT BECAUSE I STILL BELIEVE WAKANDA NEEDS ITS ROYALTY.
AND BECAUSE I KNOW THAT I AM ILL-FITTED FOR A CROWN...
...WHILE *YOU* FOUND MEANING IN THE SCEPTER.

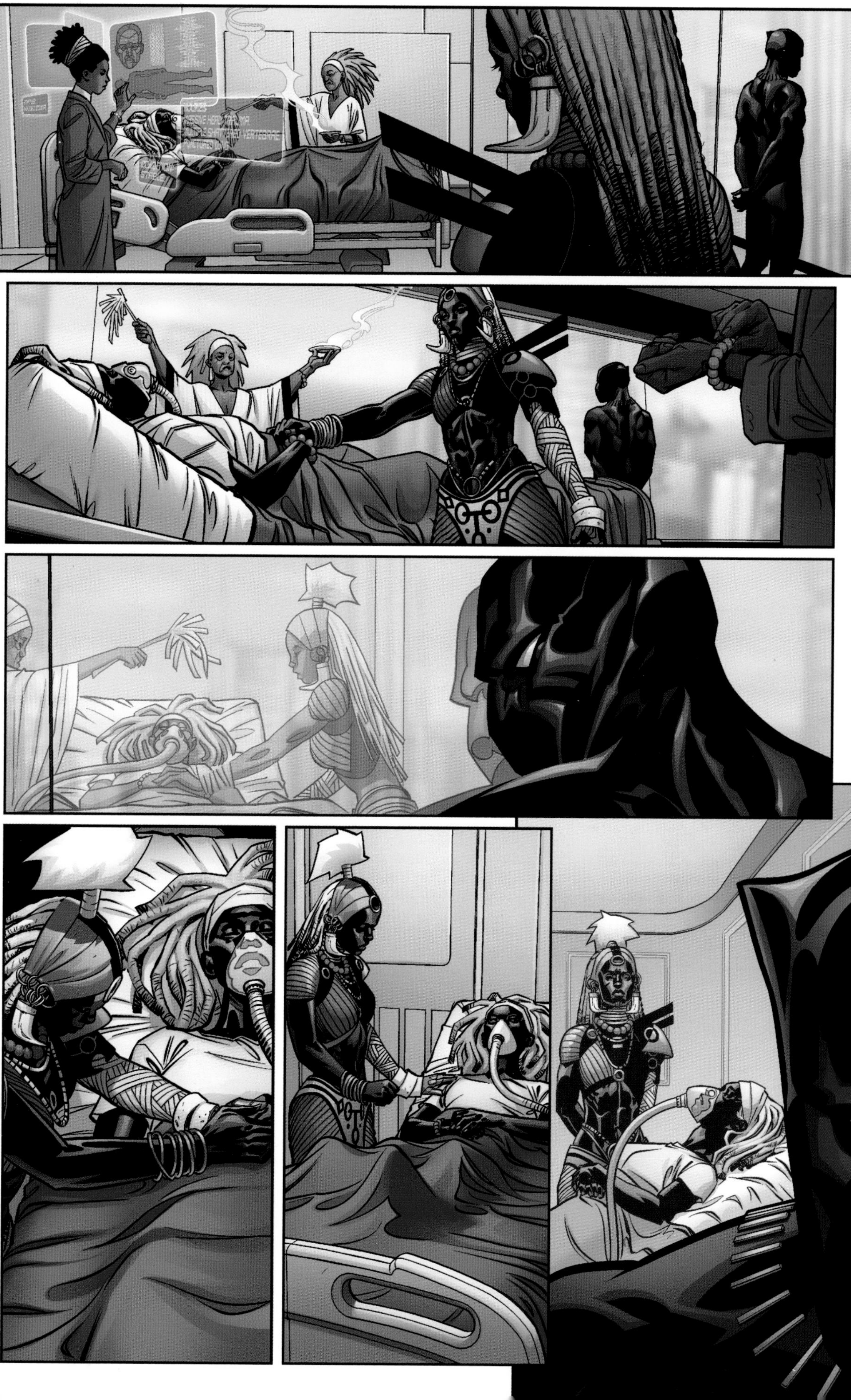
SHATTERED VERTEBRAE
STABLE

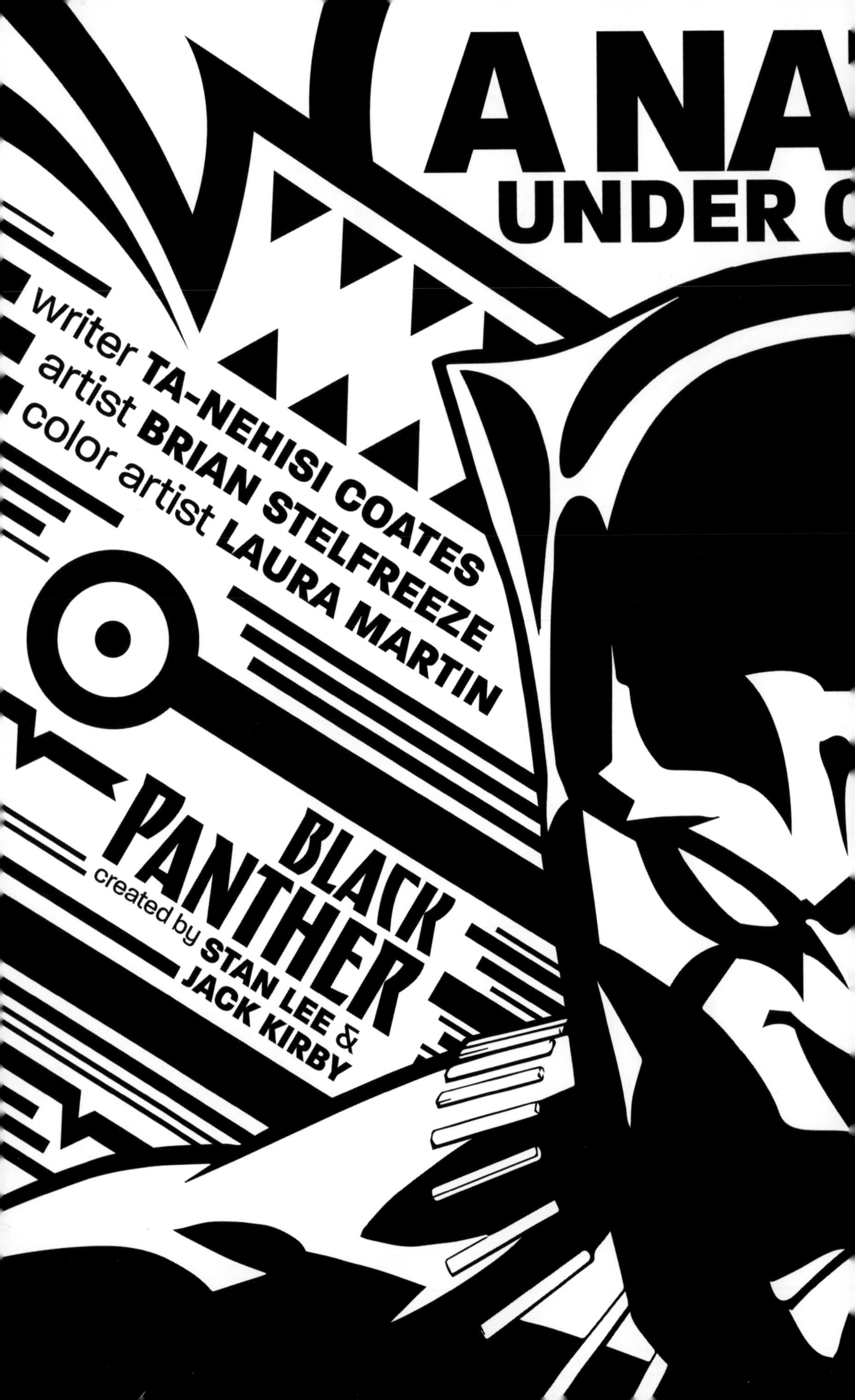
A NA
UNDER C
writer TA-NEHISI COATES
artist BRIAN STELFREEZE
color artist LAURA MARTIN
BLACK PANTHER
created by STAN LEE & JACK KIRBY

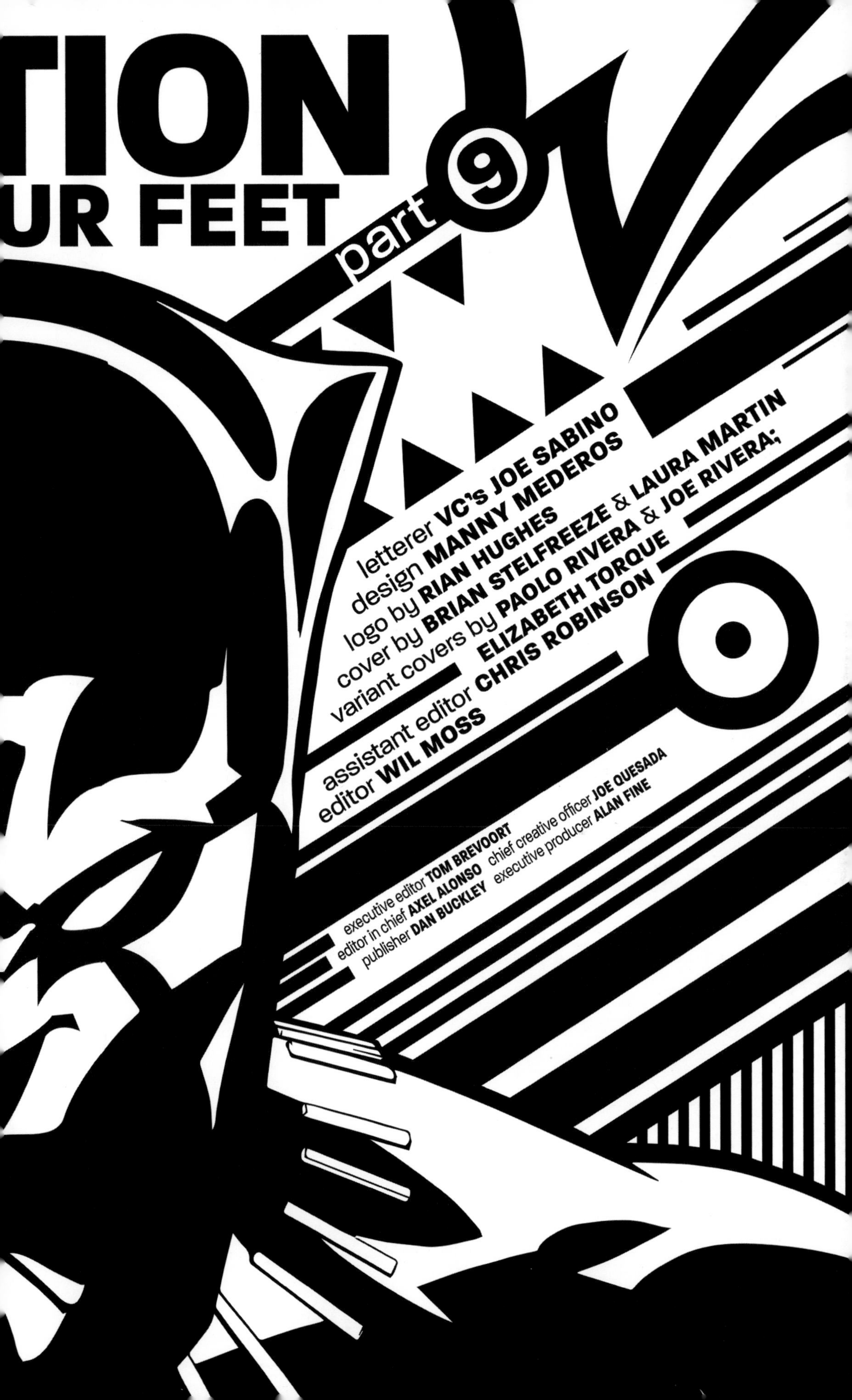
TION
UR FEET
part 9
letterer VC's JOE SABINO
design MANNY MEDEROS
logo by RIAN HUGHES
cover by BRIAN STELFREEZE & LAURA MARTIN
variant covers by PAOLO RIVERA & JOE RIVERA;
ELIZABETH TORQUE
assistant editor CHRIS ROBINSON
editor WIL MOSS
executive editor TOM BREVOORT
editor in chief AXEL ALONSO
publisher DAN BUCKLEY
chief creative officer JOE QUESADA
executive producer ALAN FINE

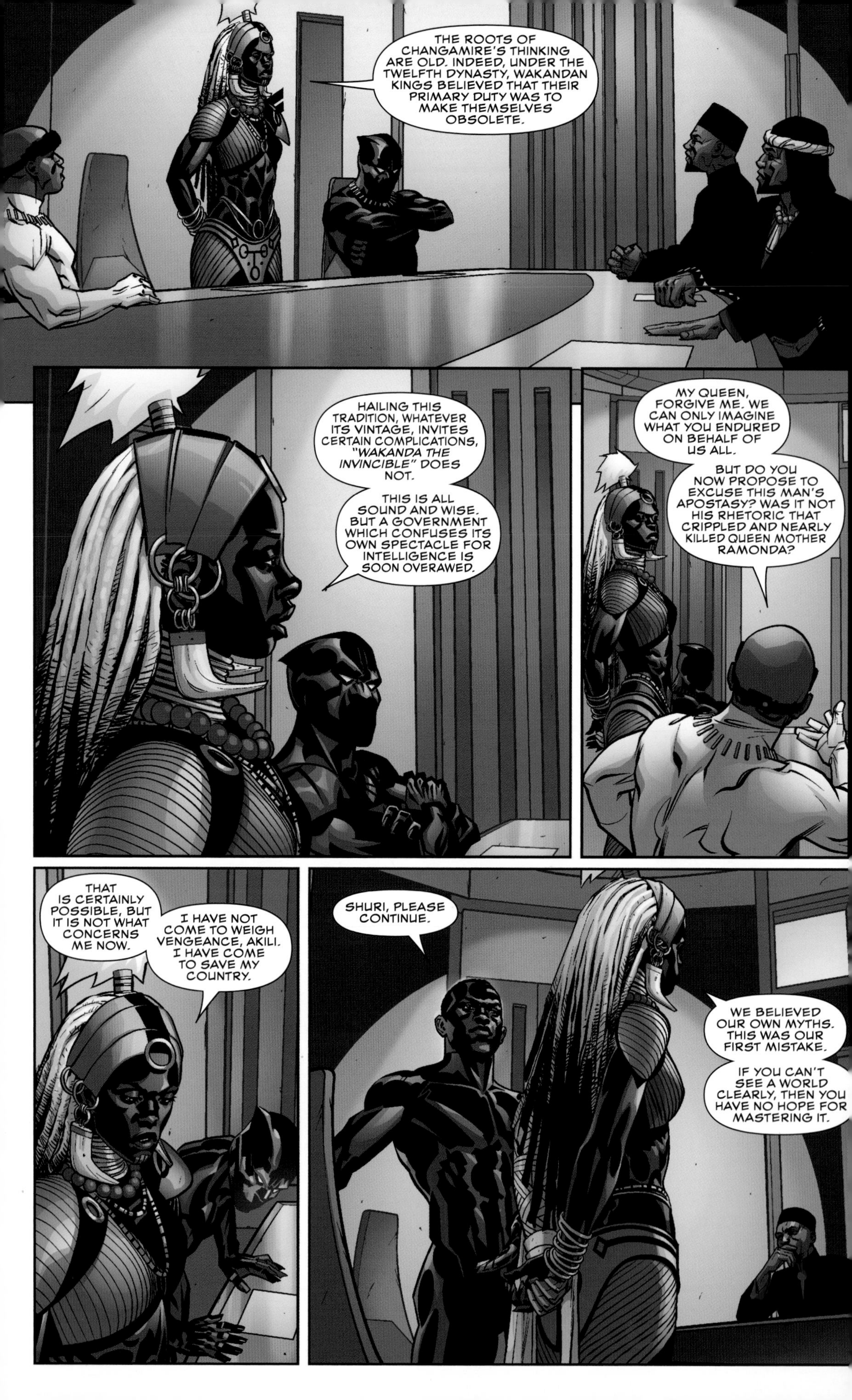
THE ROOTS OF CHANGAMIRE'S THINKING ARE OLD. INDEED, UNDER THE TWELFTH DYNASTY, WAKANDAN KINGS BELIEVED THAT THEIR PRIMARY DUTY WAS TO MAKE THEMSELVES OBSOLETE.
HAILING THIS TRADITION, WHATEVER ITS VINTAGE, INVITES CERTAIN COMPLICATIONS. "WAKANDA THE INVINCIBLE" DOES NOT.
THIS IS ALL SOUND AND WISE. BUT A GOVERNMENT WHICH CONFUSES ITS OWN SPECTACLE FOR INTELLIGENCE IS SOON OVERAWED.
MY QUEEN, FORGIVE ME. WE CAN ONLY IMAGINE WHAT YOU ENDURED ON BEHALF OF US ALL.
BUT DO YOU NOW PROPOSE TO EXCUSE THIS MAN'S APOSTASY? WAS IT NOT HIS RHETORIC THAT CRIPPLED AND NEARLY KILLED QUEEN MOTHER RAMONDA?
THAT IS CERTAINLY POSSIBLE, BUT IT IS NOT WHAT CONCERNS ME NOW.
I HAVE NOT COME TO WEIGH VENGEANCE, AKILI. I HAVE COME TO SAVE MY COUNTRY.
SHURI, PLEASE CONTINUE.
WE BELIEVED OUR OWN MYTHS. THIS WAS OUR FIRST MISTAKE.
IF YOU CAN'T SEE A WORLD CLEARLY, THEN YOU HAVE NO HOPE FOR MASTERING IT.

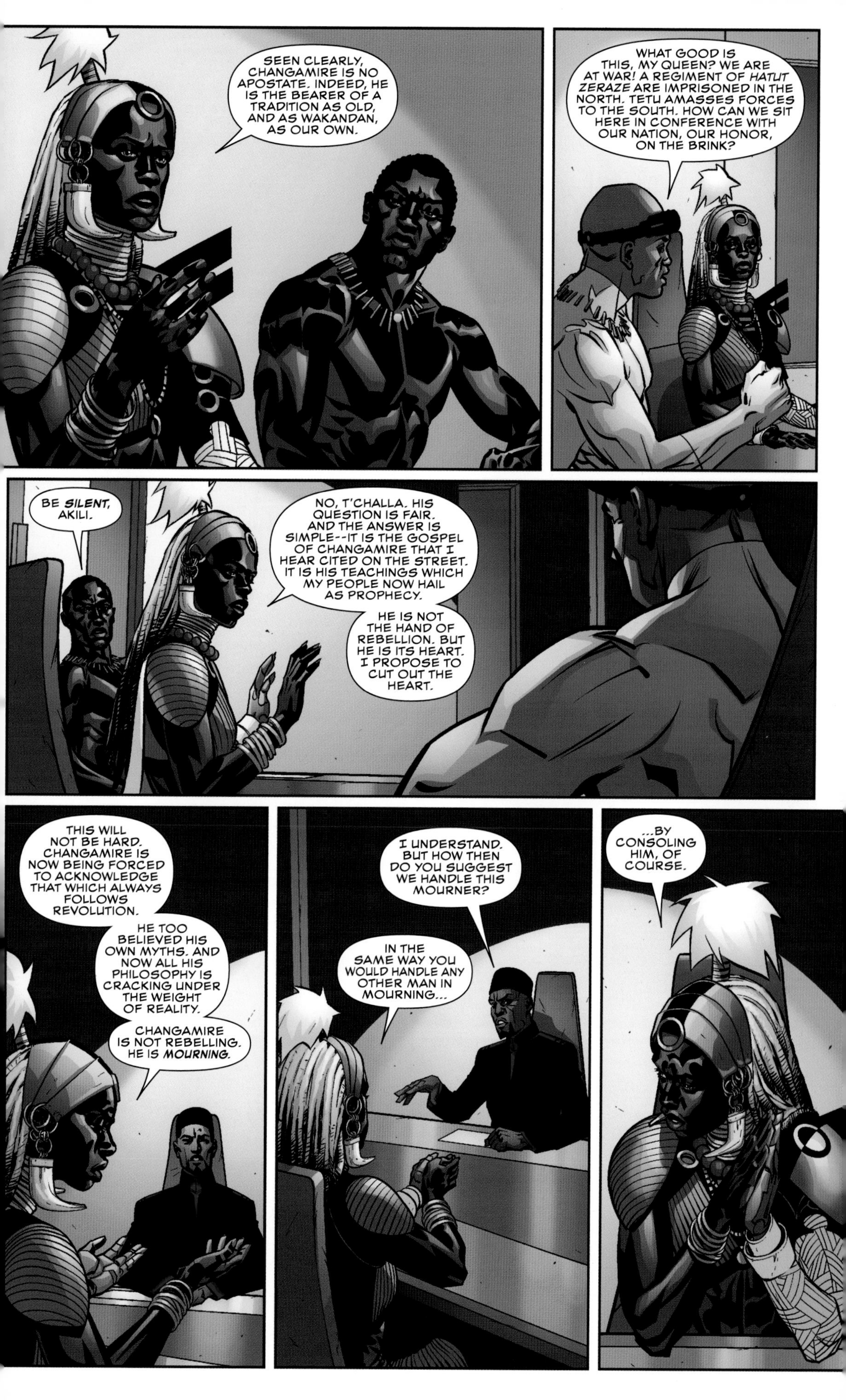
SEEN CLEARLY, CHANGAMIRE IS NO APOSTATE. INDEED, HE IS THE BEARER OF A TRADITION AS OLD, AND AS WAKANDAN, AS OUR OWN.
WHAT GOOD IS THIS, MY QUEEN? WE ARE AT WAR! A REGIMENT OF *HATUT ZERAZE* ARE IMPRISONED IN THE NORTH. TETU AMASSES FORCES TO THE SOUTH. HOW CAN WE SIT HERE IN CONFERENCE WITH OUR NATION, OUR HONOR, ON THE BRINK?
BE *SILENT*, AKILI.
NO, T'CHALLA. HIS QUESTION IS FAIR. AND THE ANSWER IS SIMPLE--IT IS THE GOSPEL OF CHANGAMIRE THAT I HEAR CITED ON THE STREET. IT IS HIS TEACHINGS WHICH MY PEOPLE NOW HAIL AS PROPHECY.
HE IS NOT THE HAND OF REBELLION. BUT HE IS ITS HEART. I PROPOSE TO CUT OUT THE HEART.
THIS WILL NOT BE HARD. CHANGAMIRE IS NOW BEING FORCED TO ACKNOWLEDGE THAT WHICH ALWAYS FOLLOWS REVOLUTION.
HE TOO BELIEVED HIS OWN MYTHS. AND NOW ALL HIS PHILOSOPHY IS CRACKING UNDER THE WEIGHT OF REALITY.
CHANGAMIRE IS NOT REBELLING. HE IS *MOURNING*.
I UNDERSTAND. BUT HOW THEN DO YOU SUGGEST WE HANDLE THIS MOURNER?
IN THE SAME WAY YOU WOULD HANDLE ANY OTHER MAN IN MOURNING...
...BY CONSOLING HIM, OF COURSE.

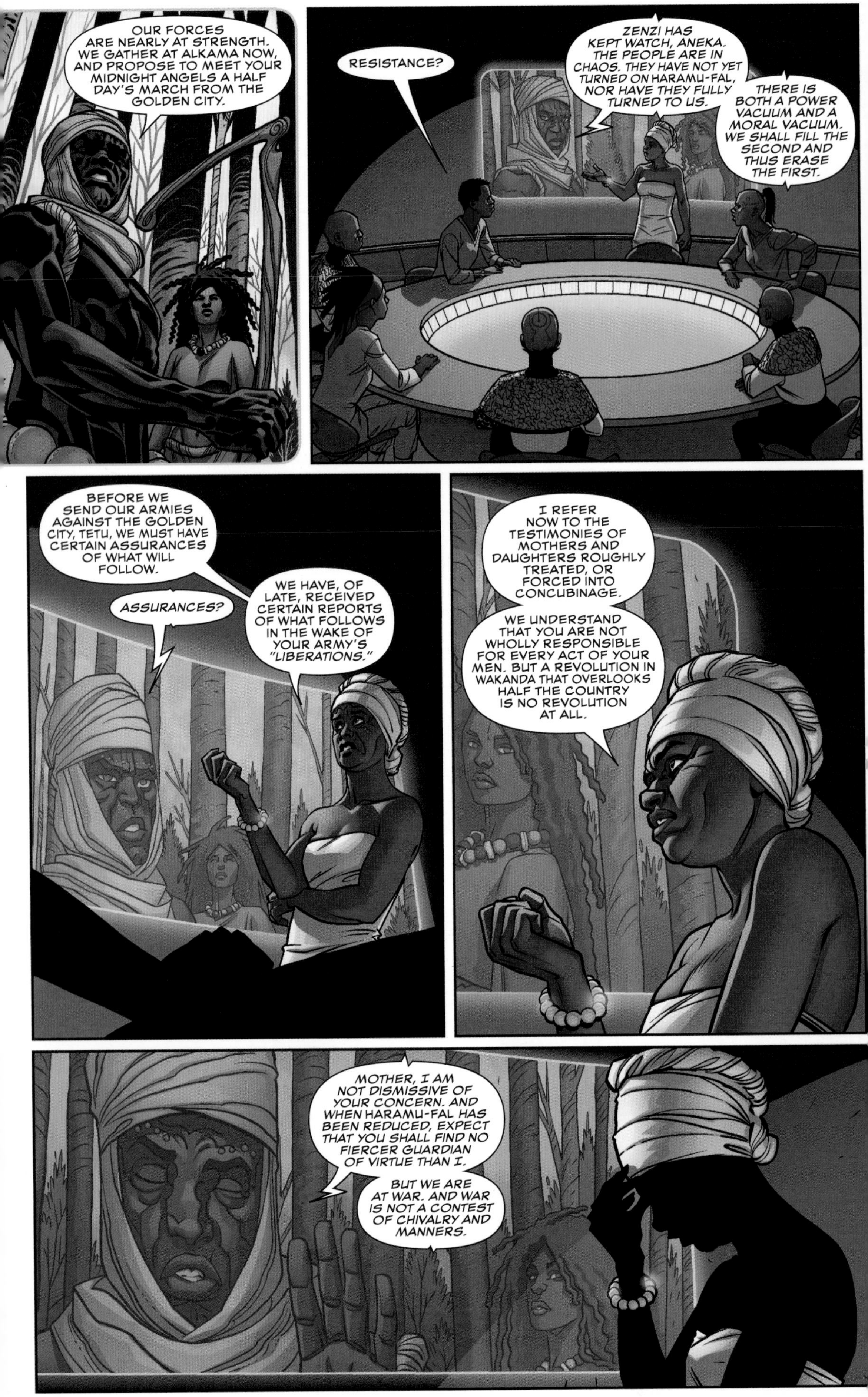
OUR FORCES ARE NEARLY AT STRENGTH. WE GATHER AT ALKAMA NOW, AND PROPOSE TO MEET YOUR MIDNIGHT ANGELS A HALF DAY'S MARCH FROM THE GOLDEN CITY.
RESISTANCE?
ZENZI HAS KEPT WATCH, ANEKA. THE PEOPLE ARE IN CHAOS. THEY HAVE NOT YET TURNED ON HARAMU-FAL, NOR HAVE THEY FULLY TURNED TO US.
THERE IS BOTH A POWER VACUUM AND A MORAL VACUUM. WE SHALL FILL THE SECOND AND THUS ERASE THE FIRST.
BEFORE WE SEND OUR ARMIES AGAINST THE GOLDEN CITY, TETU, WE MUST HAVE CERTAIN ASSURANCES OF WHAT WILL FOLLOW.
ASSURANCES?
WE HAVE, OF LATE, RECEIVED CERTAIN REPORTS OF WHAT FOLLOWS IN THE WAKE OF YOUR ARMY'S "LIBERATIONS."
I REFER NOW TO THE TESTIMONIES OF MOTHERS AND DAUGHTERS ROUGHLY TREATED, OR FORCED INTO CONCUBINAGE.
WE UNDERSTAND THAT YOU ARE NOT WHOLLY RESPONSIBLE FOR EVERY ACT OF YOUR MEN. BUT A REVOLUTION IN WAKANDA THAT OVERLOOKS HALF THE COUNTRY IS NO REVOLUTION AT ALL.
MOTHER, I AM NOT DISMISSIVE OF YOUR CONCERN. AND WHEN HARAMU-FAL HAS BEEN REDUCED, EXPECT THAT YOU SHALL FIND NO FIERCER GUARDIAN OF VIRTUE THAN I.
BUT WE ARE AT WAR. AND WAR IS NOT A CONTEST OF CHIVALRY AND MANNERS.

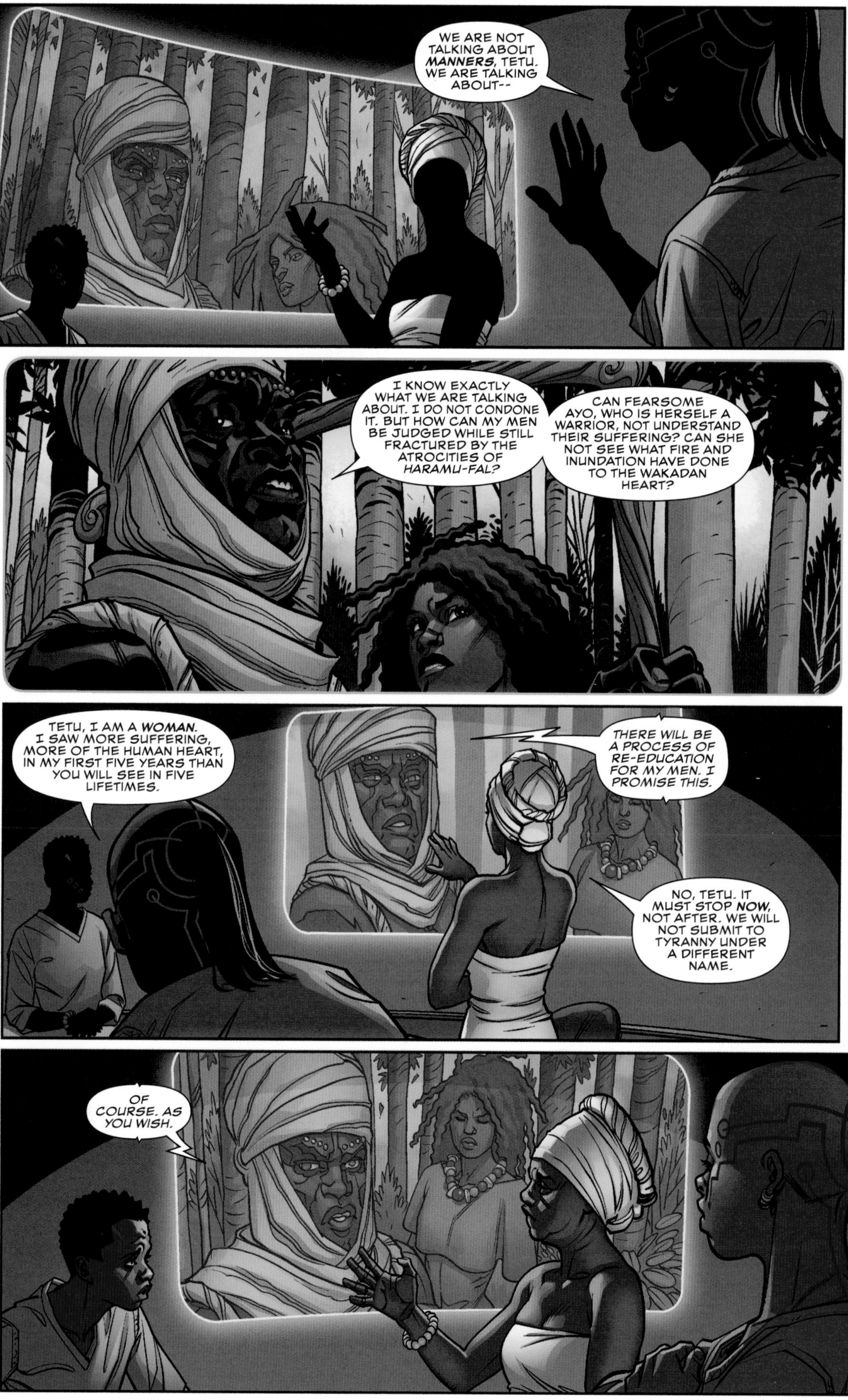
WE ARE NOT TALKING ABOUT MANNERS, TETU. WE ARE TALKING ABOUT--
I KNOW EXACTLY WHAT WE ARE TALKING ABOUT. I DO NOT CONDONE IT. BUT HOW CAN MY MEN BE JUDGED WHILE STILL FRACTURED BY THE ATROCITIES OF HARAMU-FAL?
CAN FEARSOME AYO, WHO IS HERSELF A WARRIOR, NOT UNDERSTAND THEIR SUFFERING? CAN SHE NOT SEE WHAT FIRE AND INUNDATION HAVE DONE TO THE WAKADAN HEART?
TETU, I AM A WOMAN. I SAW MORE SUFFERING, MORE OF THE HUMAN HEART, IN MY FIRST FIVE YEARS THAN YOU WILL SEE IN FIVE LIFETIMES.
THERE WILL BE A PROCESS OF RE-EDUCATION FOR MY MEN. I PROMISE THIS.
NO, TETU. IT MUST STOP NOW, NOT AFTER. WE WILL NOT SUBMIT TO TYRANNY UNDER A DIFFERENT NAME.
OF COURSE. AS YOU WISH.

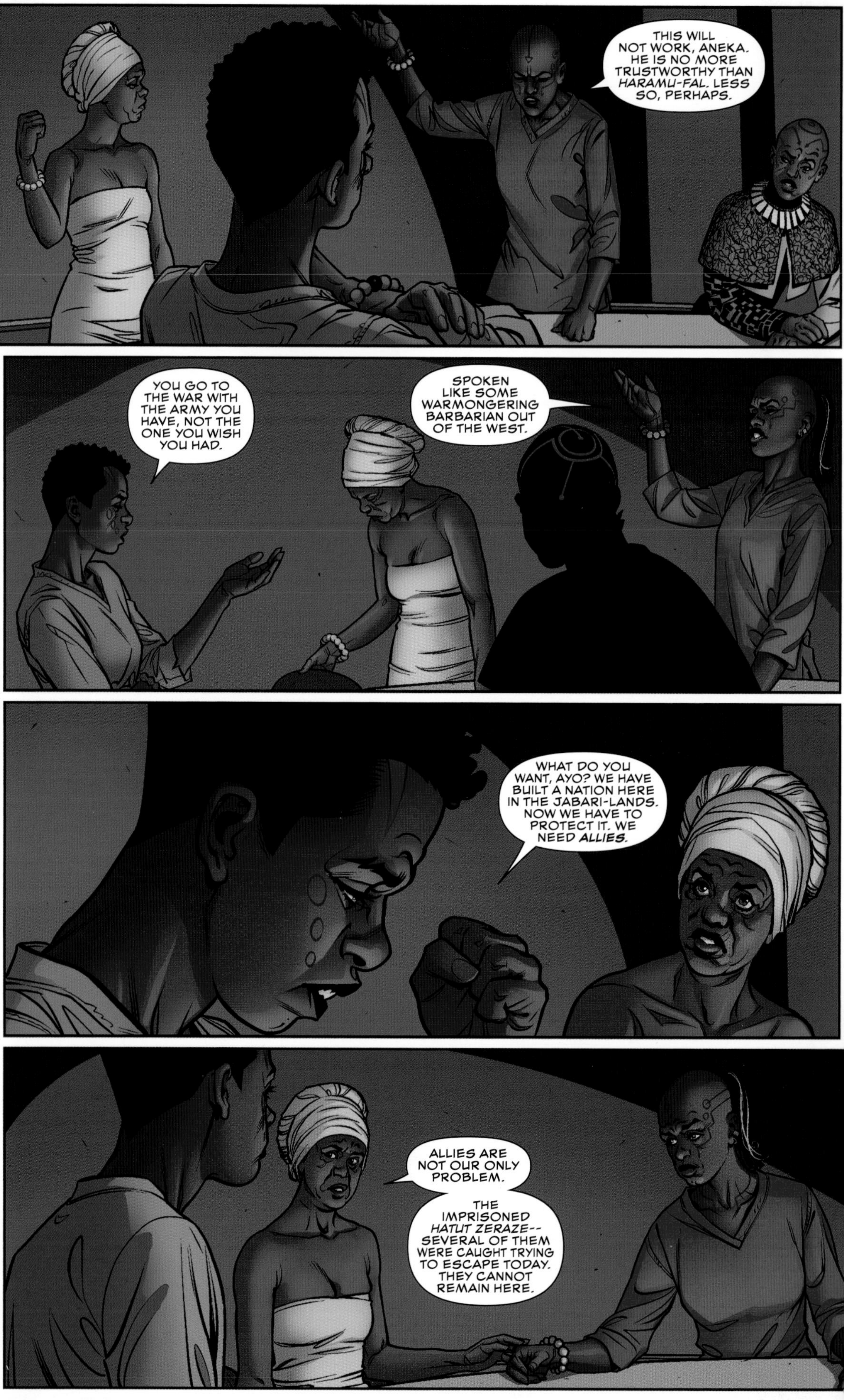

THIS WILL NOT WORK, ANEKA. HE IS NO MORE TRUSTWORTHY THAN *HARAMU-FAL*. LESS SO, PERHAPS.
YOU GO TO THE WAR WITH THE ARMY YOU HAVE, NOT THE ONE YOU WISH YOU HAD.
SPOKEN LIKE SOME WARMONGERING BARBARIAN OUT OF THE WEST.
WHAT DO YOU WANT, AYO? WE HAVE BUILT A NATION HERE IN THE JABARI-LANDS. NOW WE HAVE TO PROTECT IT. WE NEED ***ALLIES***.
ALLIES ARE NOT OUR ONLY PROBLEM.
THE IMPRISONED *HATUT ZERAZE*--SEVERAL OF THEM WERE CAUGHT TRYING TO ESCAPE TODAY. THEY CANNOT REMAIN HERE.

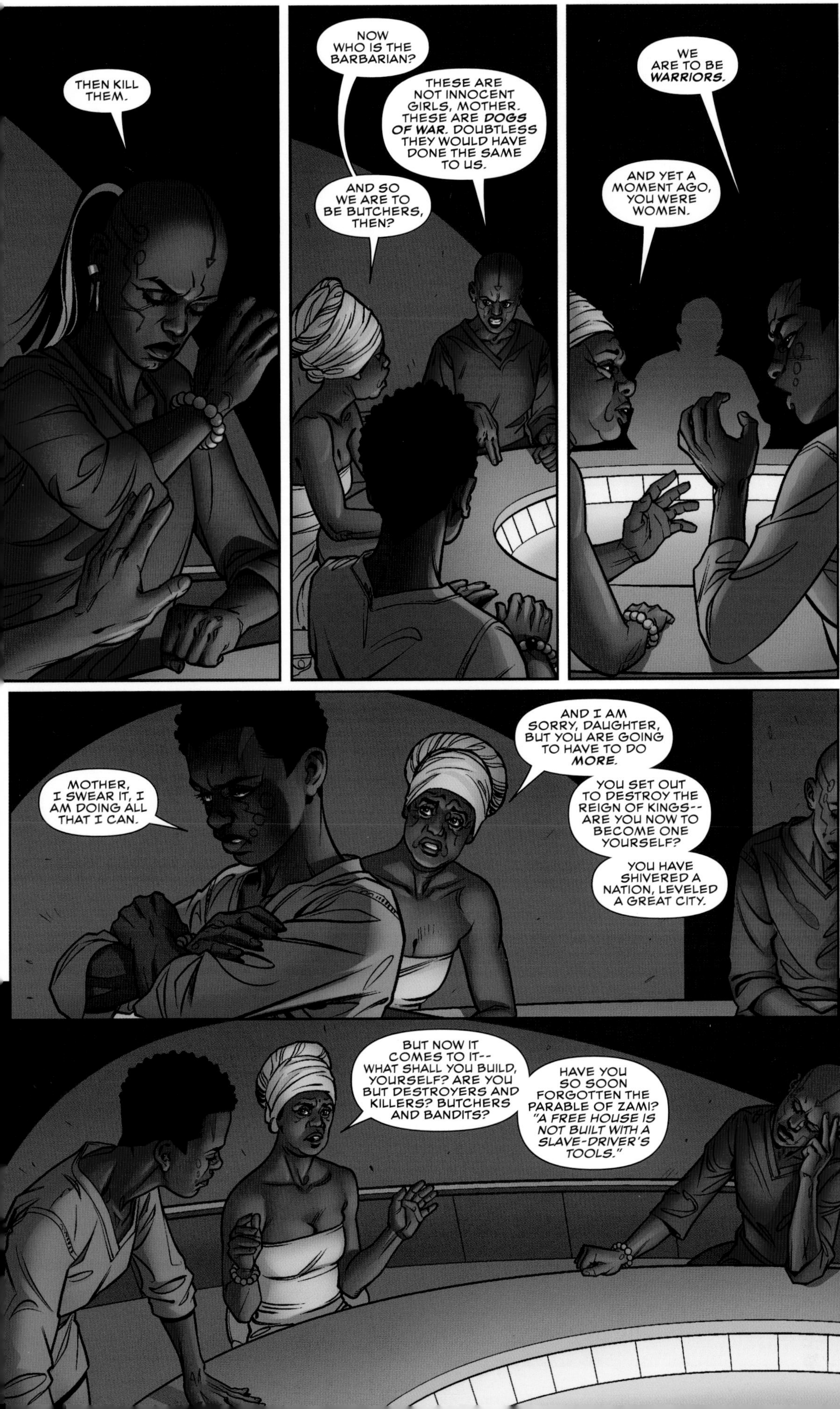
THEN KILL THEM.
NOW WHO IS THE BARBARIAN?
THESE ARE NOT INNOCENT GIRLS, MOTHER. THESE ARE DOGS OF WAR. DOUBTLESS THEY WOULD HAVE DONE THE SAME TO US.
AND SO WE ARE TO BE BUTCHERS, THEN?
WE ARE TO BE WARRIORS.
AND YET A MOMENT AGO, YOU WERE WOMEN.
MOTHER, I SWEAR IT, I AM DOING ALL THAT I CAN.
AND I AM SORRY, DAUGHTER, BUT YOU ARE GOING TO HAVE TO DO MORE.
YOU SET OUT TO DESTROY THE REIGN OF KINGS-- ARE YOU NOW TO BECOME ONE YOURSELF?
YOU HAVE SHIVERED A NATION, LEVELED A GREAT CITY.
BUT NOW IT COMES TO IT-- WHAT SHALL YOU BUILD, YOURSELF? ARE YOU BUT DESTROYERS AND KILLERS? BUTCHERS AND BANDITS?
HAVE YOU SO SOON FORGOTTEN THE PARABLE OF ZAMI? "A FREE HOUSE IS NOT BUILT WITH A SLAVE-DRIVER'S TOOLS."

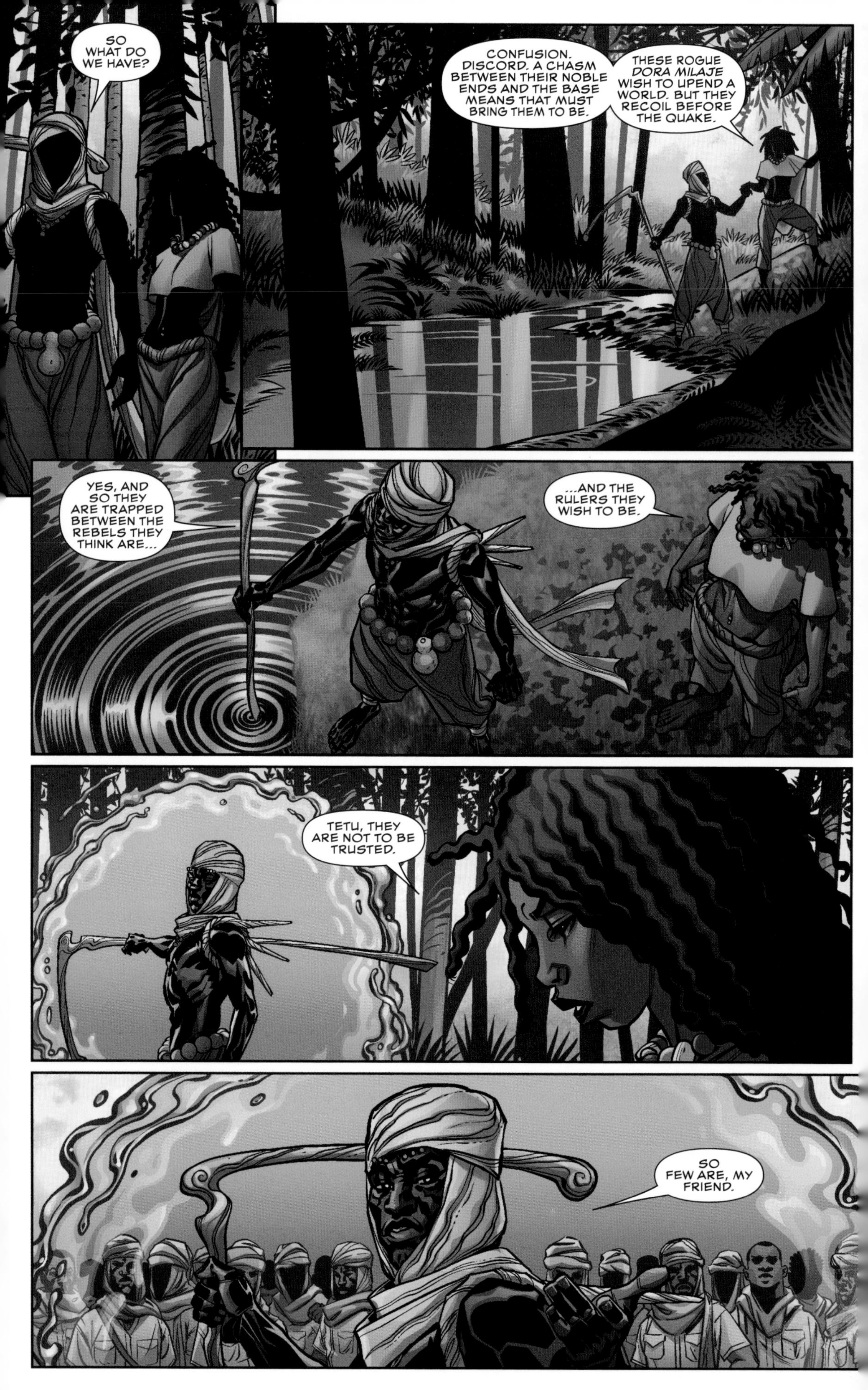
SO WHAT DO WE HAVE?
CONFUSION. DISCORD. A CHASM BETWEEN THEIR NOBLE ENDS AND THE BASE MEANS THAT MUST BRING THEM TO BE.
THESE ROGUE *DORA MILAJE* WISH TO UPEND A WORLD. BUT THEY RECOIL BEFORE THE QUAKE.
YES, AND SO THEY ARE TRAPPED BETWEEN THE REBELS THEY THINK ARE...
...AND THE RULERS THEY WISH TO BE.
TETU, THEY ARE NOT TO BE TRUSTED.
SO FEW ARE, MY FRIEND.

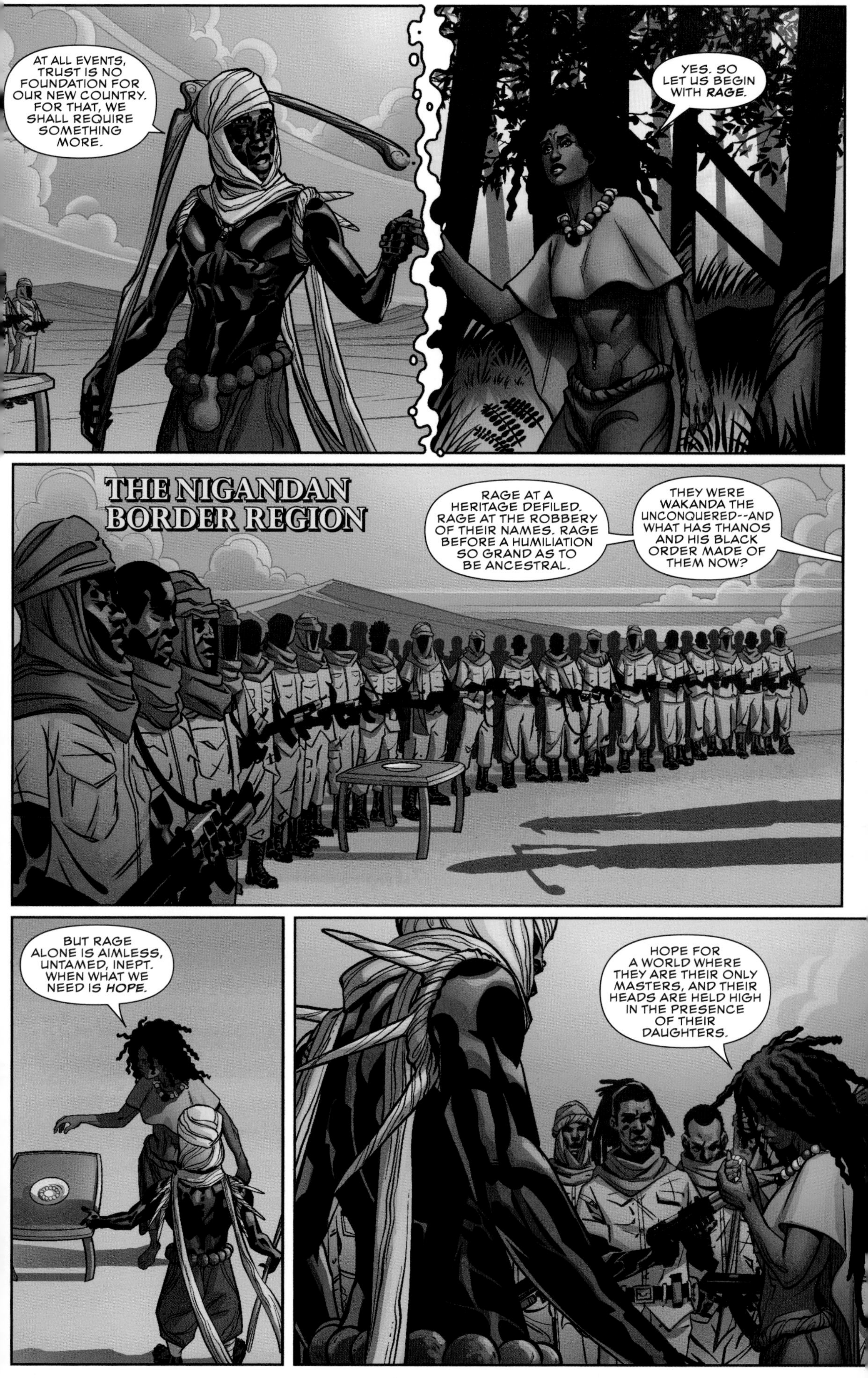
AT ALL EVENTS, TRUST IS NO FOUNDATION FOR OUR NEW COUNTRY. FOR THAT, WE SHALL REQUIRE SOMETHING MORE.
YES. SO LET US BEGIN WITH RAGE.
THE NIGANDAN BORDER REGION
RAGE AT A HERITAGE DEFILED. RAGE AT THE ROBBERY OF THEIR NAMES. RAGE BEFORE A HUMILIATION SO GRAND AS TO BE ANCESTRAL.
THEY WERE WAKANDA THE UNCONQUERED--AND WHAT HAS THANOS AND HIS BLACK ORDER MADE OF THEM NOW?
BUT RAGE ALONE IS AIMLESS, UNTAMED, INEPT. WHEN WHAT WE NEED IS HOPE.
HOPE FOR A WORLD WHERE THEY ARE THEIR ONLY MASTERS, AND THEIR HEADS ARE HELD HIGH IN THE PRESENCE OF THEIR DAUGHTERS.

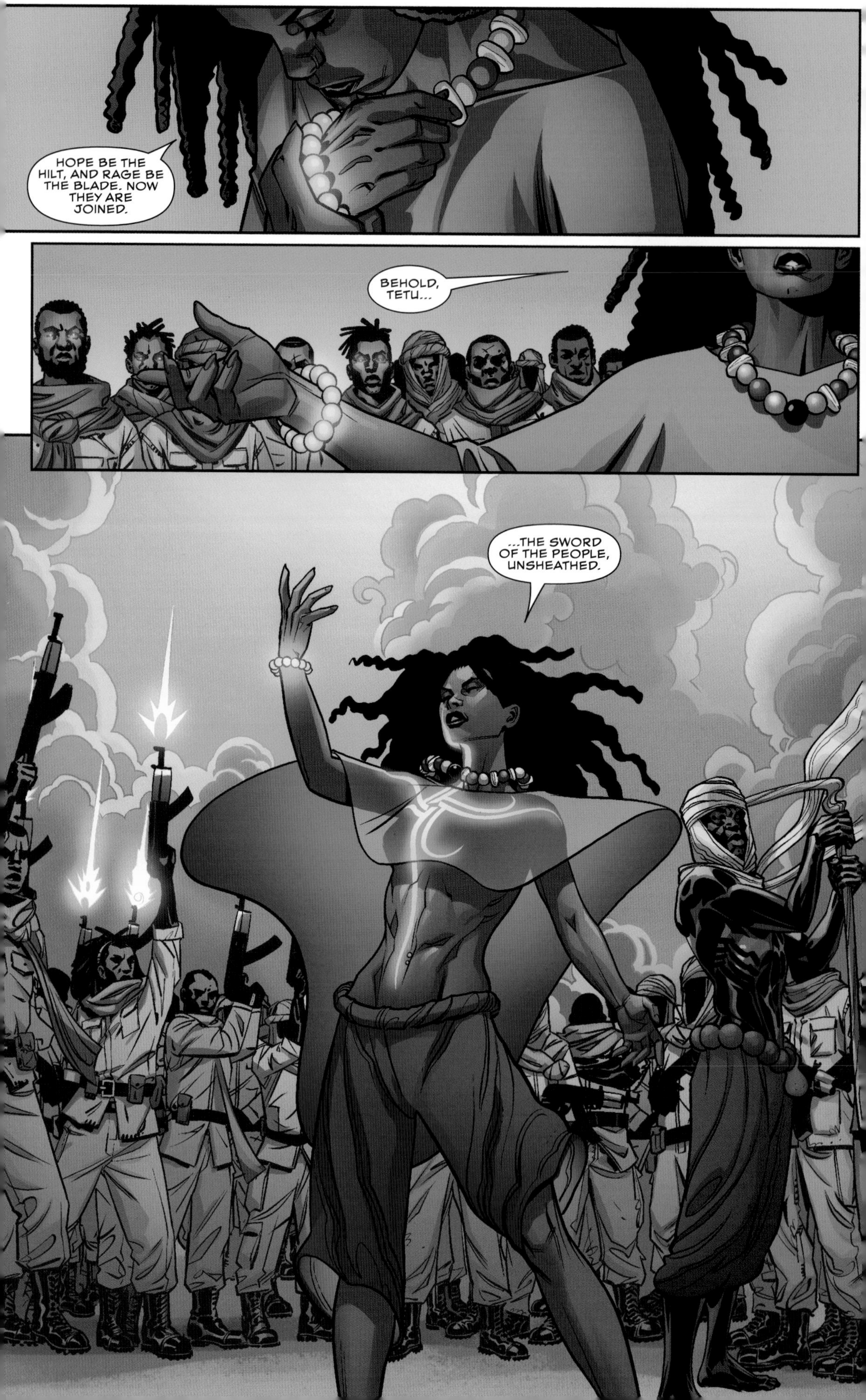
HOPE BE THE HILT, AND RAGE BE THE BLADE. NOW THEY ARE JOINED.
BEHOLD, TETU...
...THE SWORD OF THE PEOPLE, UNSHEATHED.

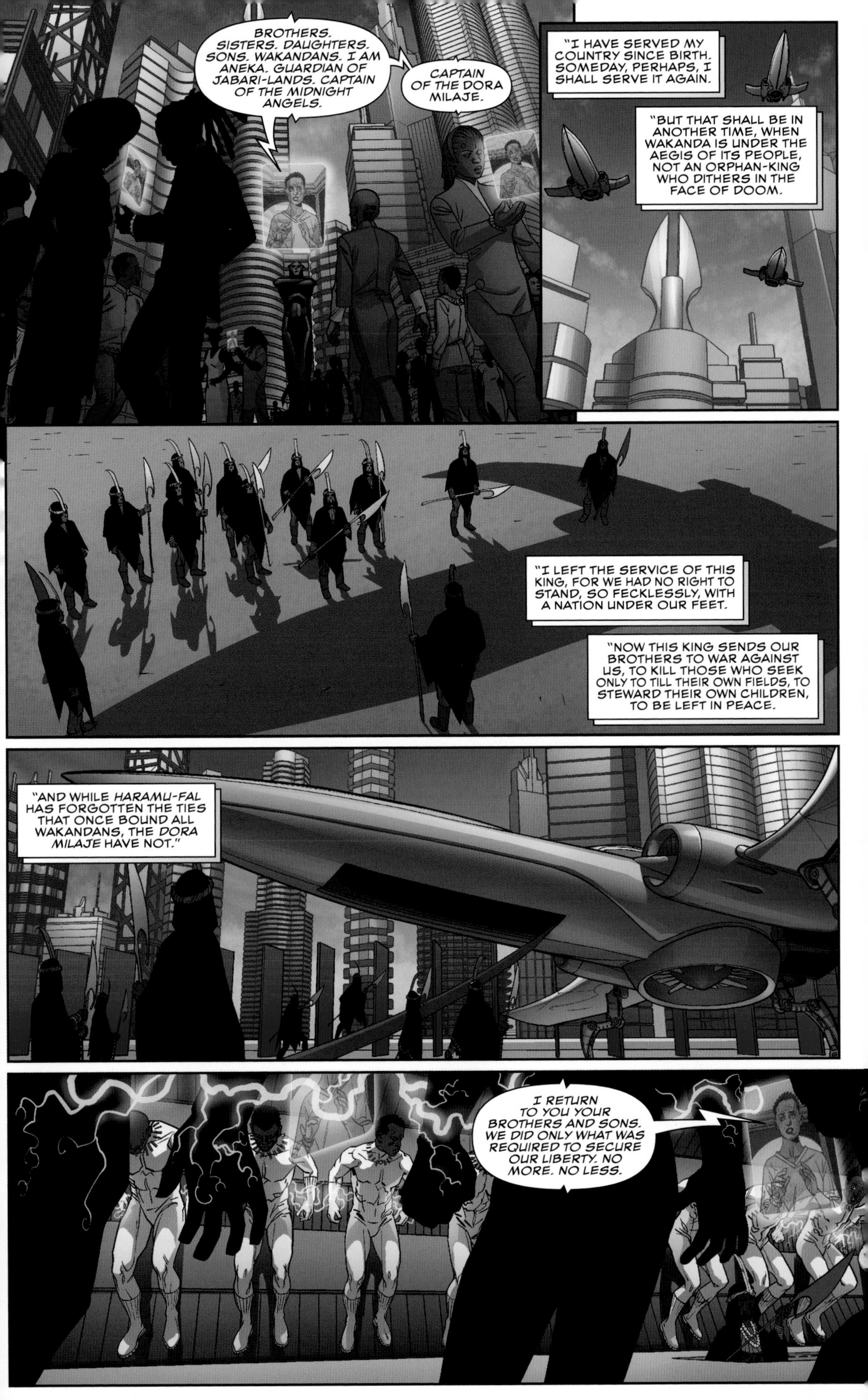
BROTHERS. SISTERS. DAUGHTERS. SONS. WAKANDANS. I AM ANEKA. GUARDIAN OF JABARI-LANDS. CAPTAIN OF THE MIDNIGHT ANGELS.
CAPTAIN OF THE DORA MILAJE.
"I HAVE SERVED MY COUNTRY SINCE BIRTH. SOMEDAY, PERHAPS, I SHALL SERVE IT AGAIN.
"BUT THAT SHALL BE IN ANOTHER TIME, WHEN WAKANDA IS UNDER THE AEGIS OF ITS PEOPLE, NOT AN ORPHAN-KING WHO DITHERS IN THE FACE OF DOOM.
"I LEFT THE SERVICE OF THIS KING, FOR WE HAD NO RIGHT TO STAND, SO FECKLESSLY, WITH A NATION UNDER OUR FEET.
"NOW THIS KING SENDS OUR BROTHERS TO WAR AGAINST US, TO KILL THOSE WHO SEEK ONLY TO TILL THEIR OWN FIELDS, TO STEWARD THEIR OWN CHILDREN, TO BE LEFT IN PEACE.
"AND WHILE HARAMU-FAL HAS FORGOTTEN THE TIES THAT ONCE BOUND ALL WAKANDANS, THE DORA MILAJE HAVE NOT."
I RETURN TO YOU YOUR BROTHERS AND SONS. WE DID ONLY WHAT WAS REQUIRED TO SECURE OUR LIBERTY. NO MORE. NO LESS.

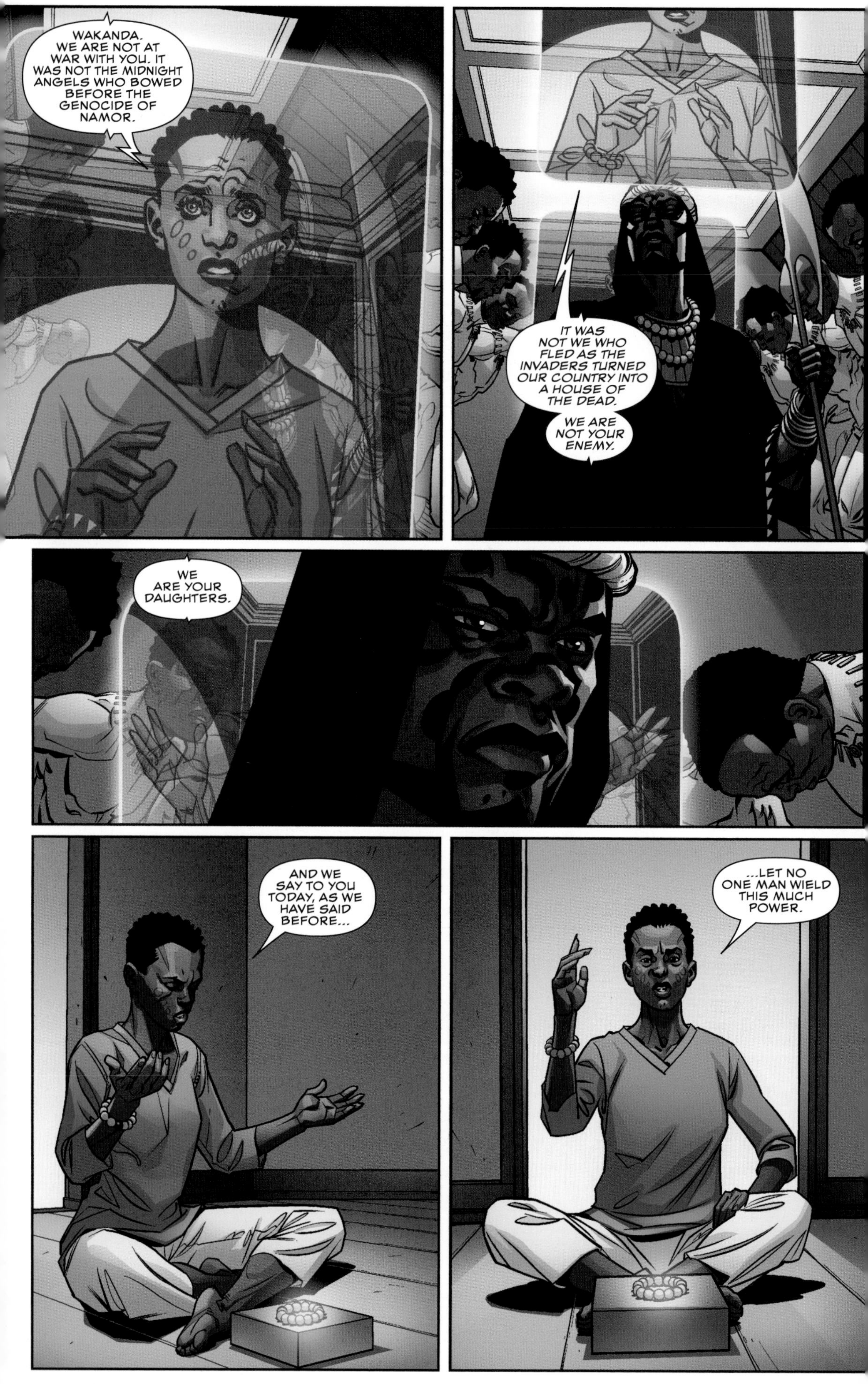
WAKANDA. WE ARE NOT AT WAR WITH YOU. IT WAS NOT THE MIDNIGHT ANGELS WHO BOWED BEFORE THE GENOCIDE OF NAMOR.
IT WAS NOT WE WHO FLED AS THE INVADERS TURNED OUR COUNTRY INTO A HOUSE OF THE DEAD.
WE ARE NOT YOUR ENEMY.
WE ARE YOUR DAUGHTERS.
AND WE SAY TO YOU TODAY, AS WE HAVE SAID BEFORE...
...LET NO ONE MAN WIELD THIS MUCH POWER.

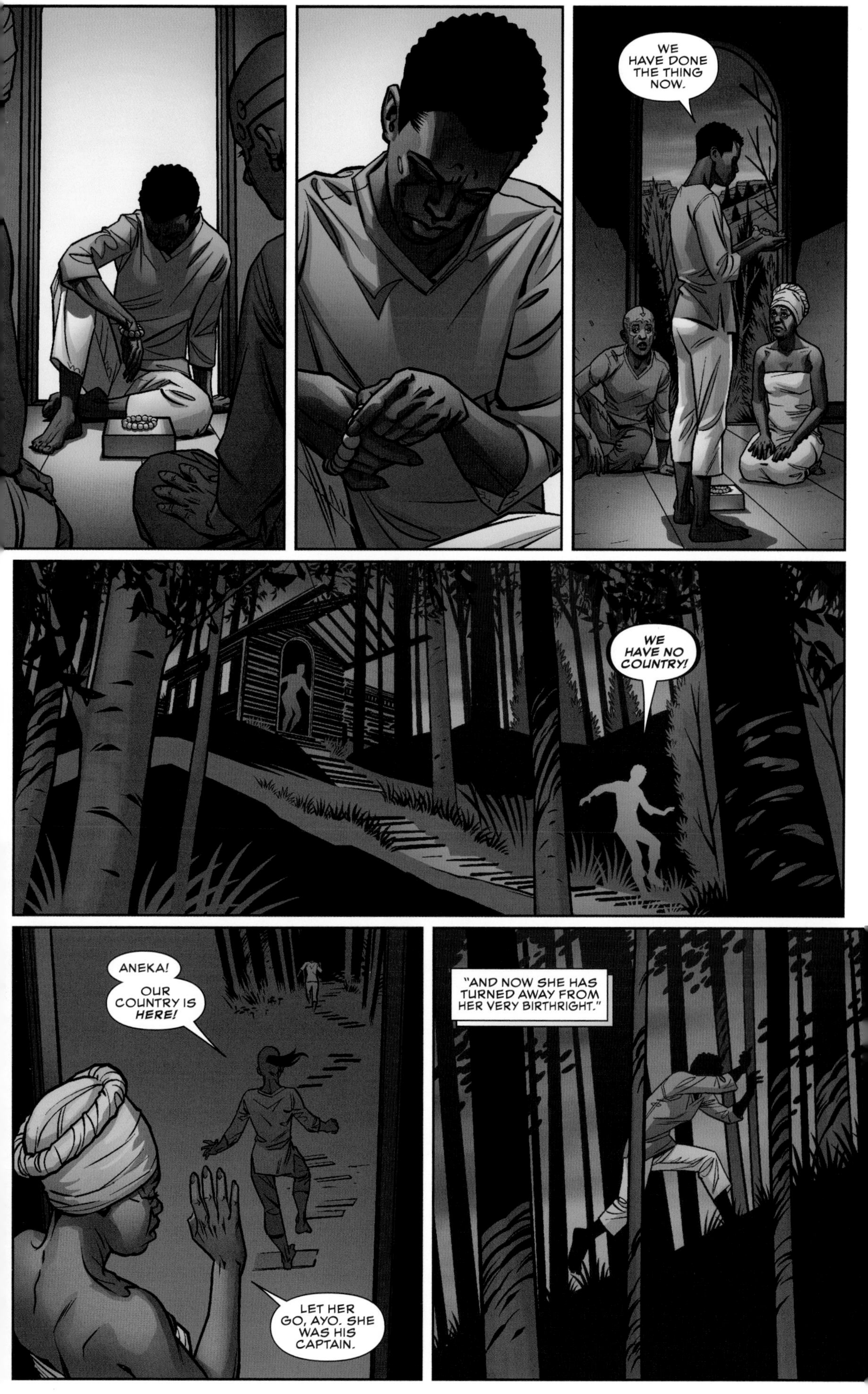
WE HAVE DONE THE THING NOW.
WE HAVE NO COUNTRY!
ANEKA!
OUR COUNTRY IS HERE!
LET HER GO, AYO. SHE WAS HIS CAPTAIN.
"AND NOW SHE HAS TURNED AWAY FROM HER VERY BIRTHRIGHT."

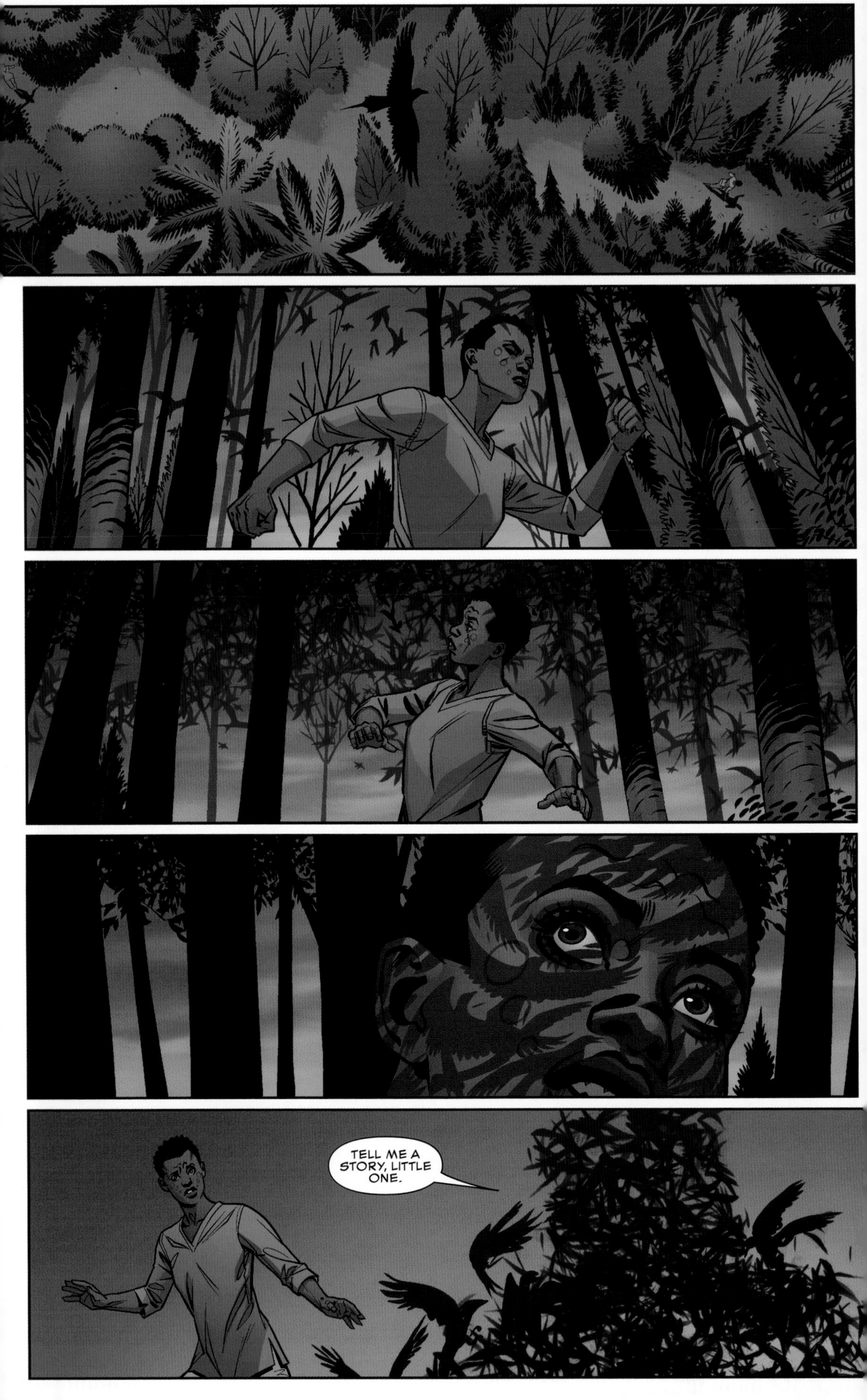
TELL ME A STORY, LITTLE ONE.

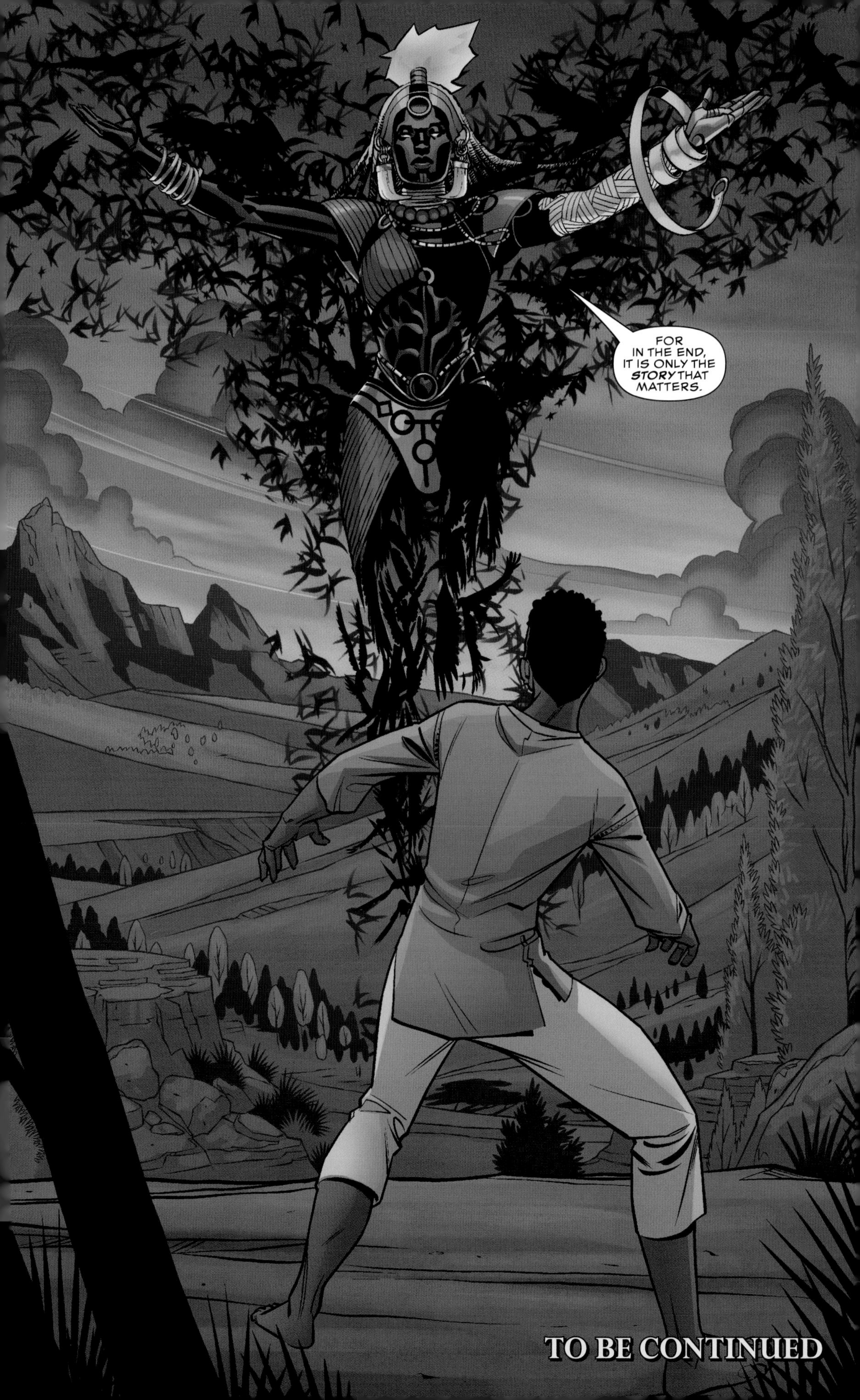
FOR IN THE END, IT IS ONLY THE STORY THAT MATTERS.
TO BE CONTINUED

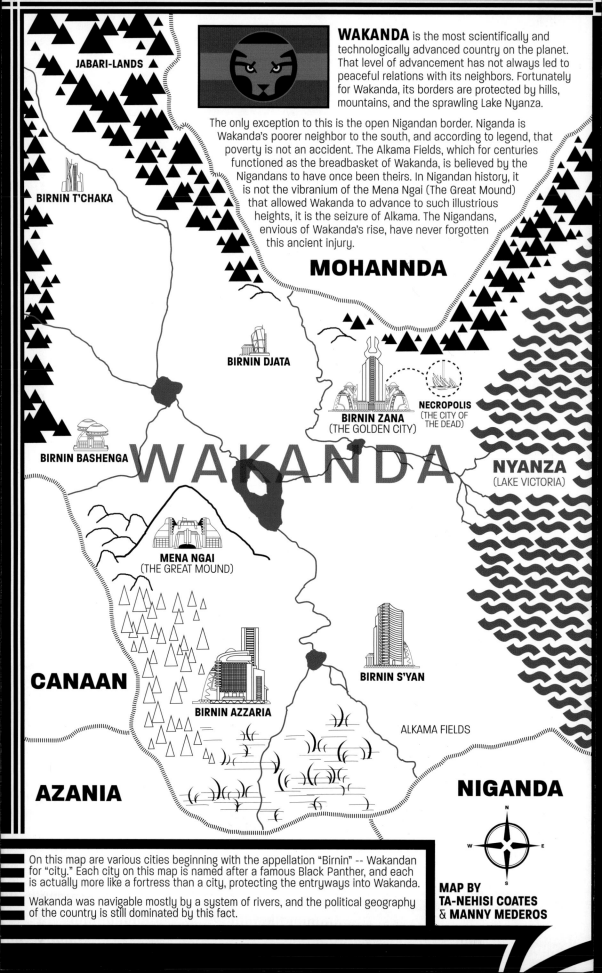

WAKANDA is the most scientifically and technologically advanced country on the planet. That level of advancement has not always led to peaceful relations with its neighbors. Fortunately for Wakanda, its borders are protected by hills, mountains, and the sprawling Lake Nyanza.

The only exception to this is the open Nigandan border. Niganda is Wakanda's poorer neighbor to the south, and according to legend, that poverty is not an accident. The Alkama Fields, which for centuries functioned as the breadbasket of Wakanda, is believed by the Nigandans to have once been theirs. In Nigandan history, it is not the vibranium of the Mena Ngai (The Great Mound) that allowed Wakanda to advance to such illustrious heights, it is the seizure of Alkama. The Nigandans, envious of Wakanda's rise, have never forgotten this ancient injury.

JABARI-LANDS

BIRNIN T'CHAKA

MOHANNDA

BIRNIN DJATA

BIRNIN ZANA
(THE GOLDEN CITY)

NECROPOLIS
(THE CITY OF THE DEAD)

BIRNIN BASHENGA

WAKANDA

NYANZA
(LAKE VICTORIA)

MENA NGAI
(THE GREAT MOUND)

CANAAN

BIRNIN S'YAN

BIRNIN AZZARIA

ALKAMA FIELDS

AZANIA

NIGANDA

On this map are various cities beginning with the appellation "Birnin" -- Wakandan for "city." Each city on this map is named after a famous Black Panther, and each is actually more like a fortress than a city, protecting the entryways into Wakanda.

Wakanda was navigable mostly by a system of rivers, and the political geography of the country is still dominated by this fact.

**MAP BY
TA-NEHISI COATES
& MANNY MEDEROS**

BLACK PANTHER

BLACK PANTHER

COLLECT THEM ALL!

Set of 6 Hardcover Books ISBN: 978-1-5321-4777-7

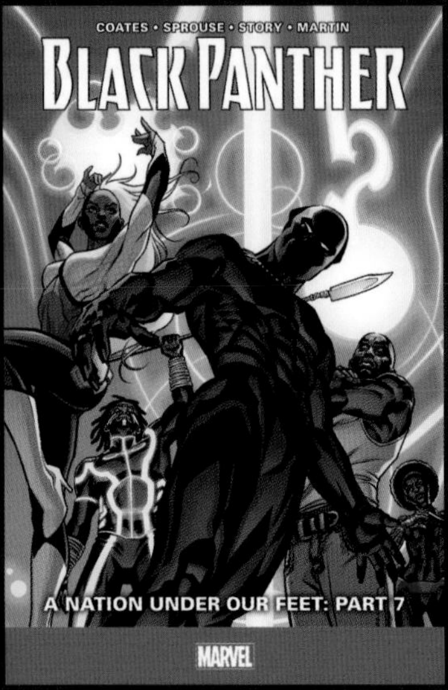
COATES • SPROUSE • STORY • MARTIN
BLACK PANTHER
A NATION UNDER OUR FEET: PART 7
MARVEL

Hardcover Book ISBN
978-1-5321-4778-4

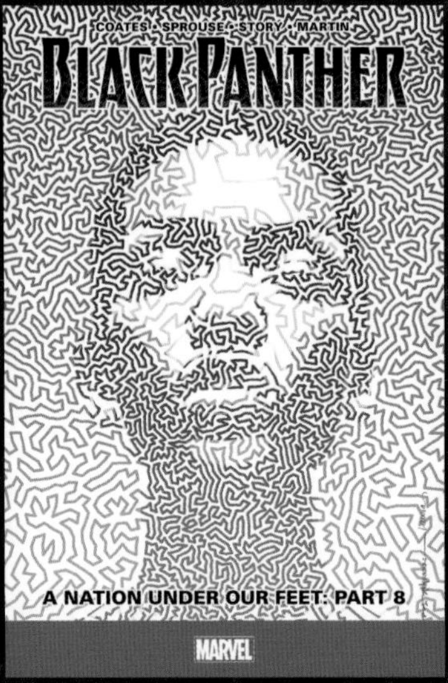
COATES • SPROUSE • STORY • MARTIN
BLACK PANTHER
A NATION UNDER OUR FEET: PART 8
MARVEL

Hardcover Book ISBN
978-1-5321-4779-1

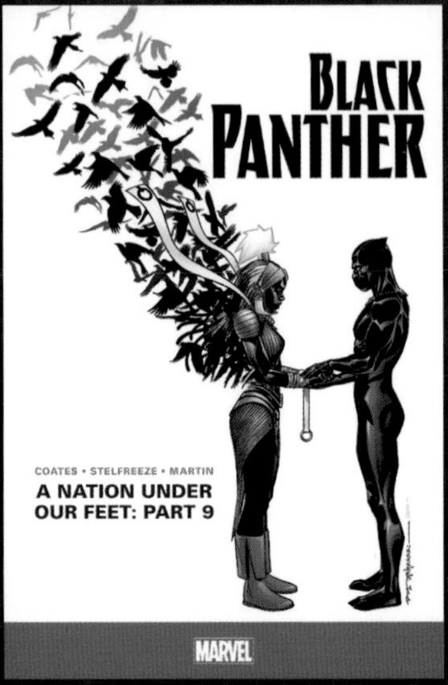
BLACK PANTHER
COATES • STELFREEZE • MARTIN
A NATION UNDER OUR FEET: PART 9
MARVEL

Hardcover Book ISBN
978-1-5321-4780-7

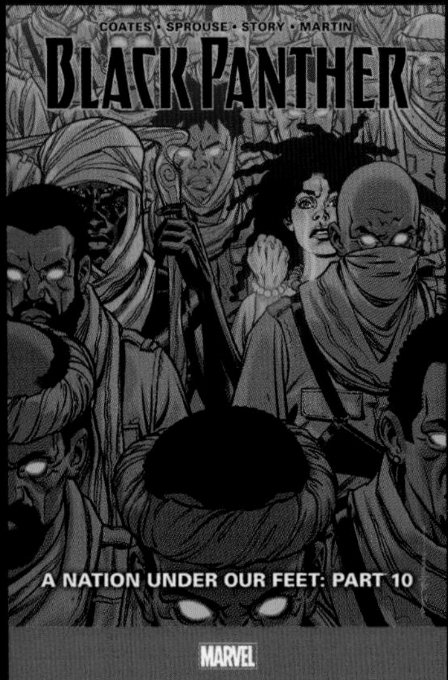
COATES • SPROUSE • STORY • MARTIN
BLACK PANTHER
A NATION UNDER OUR FEET: PART 10
MARVEL

Hardcover Book ISBN
978-1-5321-4781-4

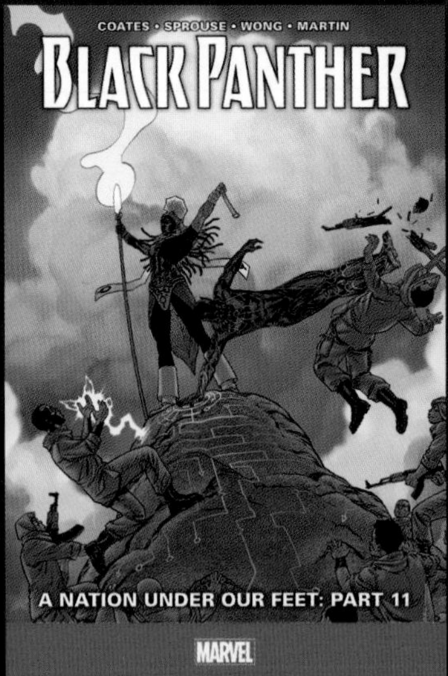
COATES • SPROUSE • WONG • MARTIN
BLACK PANTHER
A NATION UNDER OUR FEET: PART 11
MARVEL

Hardcover Book ISBN
978-1-5321-4782-1

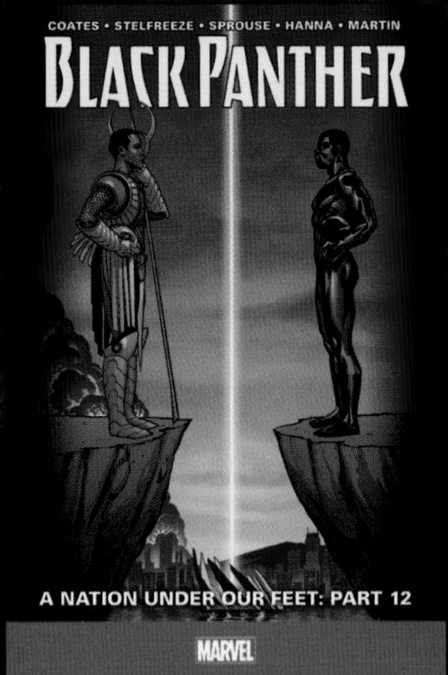
COATES • STELFREEZE • SPROUSE • HANNA • MARTIN
BLACK PANTHER
A NATION UNDER OUR FEET: PART 12
MARVEL

Hardcover Book ISBN
978-1-5321-4783-8